# THE OATH

## An Extreme Introduction to Her New Career

Sybil Norcroft Book Nine

## CARL DOUGLASS

Neurosurgeon Turned Author
Who Writes With Gripping Realism

PUBLICATION
CONSULTANTS
We Believe In The Power Of Authors

*PO Box 221974 Anchorage, Alaska 99522-1974*
*books@publicationconsultants.com, www.publicationconsultants.com*

ISBN Number: 978-1-63747-002-2
eBook ISBN Number: 978-1-63747-003-9

Library of Congress Number: 2021930242

Manufactured in the United States of America

# CHAPTER ONE

During the flight from Utah back to Washington DC, Sybil Norcroft–who would be the next president if she survived the flight–had a long time to think about what all of it meant. She had been appointed as vice-president for President Parker Conrad Willets only a few months ago to take the place of the man who had disgraced the office—Randall Broome. For the rest of the world, that man had died and was interned in Arlington National Cemetery with full honors. That was a fiction to hide the fact of his horrific crimes and to start the nation on a track to healing. Sybil–acting in her capacity as the new (emergency) vice-president and also as the director of the Central Intelligence Agency– had personally seen to it that the man—also known as Beelzebub the Magnificent—never saw or was seen by the public again, or that his very existence was persisting.

She had been warned that the death of her predecessor, President Willets, was pending, but not as suddenly as it happened. He was just over two years into his second term in office. The secret service agents who came for her and were flying her to the capital had told her that she was the new president, a great shock to her and her family. That, she knew—was not quite a completed fact—since she had not taken the oath of office. For that reason, she was being rushed to Washington for a meeting with the Chief Justice of the Supreme Court.

Her thoughts were jumbled and all over the map. She knew she had to get control, and she had to do so in less than four hours. She had had a career which prepared her to handle even such momentous occurrences as this one. She finished her university undergraduate career with top honors, despite what she considered to be blatant favoritism shone to her male competitors. As a result, she became a prominent feminist—and, for a time—was president of the nation's most prominent activist organization. She graduated from medical school with high honors and was the valedictorian. She completed a prestigious neurosurgery residency and became the head of the department in her private hospital.

She became a fellow of the American College of Surgeons, and, after her neurosurgery residency, a fellow of the American Association of Neurological Surgeons. She extended her education even though she was in active practice until she received a PhD. Had she desired to do so, she could have used an impressive set of initials after her name: BS (Bachelor of Science—Medical Studies), FACS (Fellow of the American College of Surgeons), PhD (Neurological Systems Studies), and FAANS (Fellow of the American Association of Neurosurgeons).

Life challenges led her career to a Y in the road. For important reasons–mostly beyond her control–Sybil chose to become the chief medical consultant for Wolf News and worked her way up to a spot as a prime-time anchor. Along the way up that ladder, she was recruited as a CIA agent and ended up as the DCIA. That gave her access to a world of secrets and of adventures as an active field agent. More significantly, it brought her into regular contact with the late president.

The helicopter touched down at the Andrews Air Force Base helipad where a shining black limousine was waiting. There were two more secret service agents; so, when she and her two minders from the helicopter got into the limo, the full complement of presidential security was present. They sped—lights and sirens–the twenty miles northwest through the evening rush hour traffic from Andrews AFB via I-495 s/I-95 S to Alexandria, then I-395, then the 12th St. Expressway and Constitution Avenue NW to 16th St. NW, then on Ellipse Road NW to 1600 Pennsylvania Avenue NW. The White House security gate was awaiting their arrival.

The chief usher Walter Crockett and an additional two secret service agents moved Sybil and her entourage—now nine people—quickly to the Oval Office in the West Wing where a small group of dignitaries and White House secretaries and photographers were waiting. Most of them were there to serve as witnesses. The Speaker of the House, Senate Majority Leader, Chief Justice of the Supreme Court, and a US Army major in full dress uniform holding a heavy brief case, stood when Sybil was escorted into the room. It was a somber scene; several of the people had obviously been weeping. Sybil felt lonely, entirely out of place among these august figures, several of whom barely recognized her.

"Madam Vice-President, please sit here behind the Resolute Desk and place your left hand on the Bible and bring your right hand to the square. I am directed by the Constitution of the United States, Article II, Section 1, to administer the Oath of Office."

She did so.

"Repeat after me: 'I, Sybil Norcroft Daniels, do solemnly affirm that I will faithfully execute the office of President of the United States, and will, to the best of my ability, preserve, protect, and defend the Constitution of the United States. So help me God.'"

"Let me be the first to congratulate you, Madam President," Chief Justice Chester Whitfield said and gave her a welcoming smile.

Everyone in the room except the army major shook her hand and offered her congratulations. Several added that they wished this occasion had come in the ordinary course of transition of presidencies, but this was not ordinary. In a few days, the nation would bury a former president; but today it would have to begin to know a new one.

For a few moments, Sybil remained seated behind the Oval Office desk, alone except for the army major holding the "football". Under existing federal law and custom, major-party presidential candidates become eligible to receive classified national security briefings once their nomination is formalized at the party's national convention. Transition services are designed under the law to involve key personnel from the outgoing and incoming presidents' staffs, and a host of activities, such as vetting candidates for positions in the new administration, helping to familiarize the incoming administration with the operations of the executive branch, and developing a comprehensive policy platform—all in the months and days before inauguration.

It is expected that—during the pre-election and pre-inauguration phases–considerable planning and arrangements will be accomplished: setting goals for the transition; assembling and organizing the key transition team staff; allocating responsibilities among the team and allocating resources and personnel for each core work stream; developing an overall management work plan to guide the team through the entire transition process; and establishing relationships with Congress, the outgoing administration, General Services Administration, the Office of Government Ethics, the FBI, and the Office of Personnel Management to encourage information sharing and to begin the security clearance process for select personnel. None of that had happened; no one was really prepared for Sybil Norcroft-Daniels to be president, and she admitted to herself that she was probably the least prepared.

There was no transition team to handle the expected influx of campaign staff and personnel who then had to be trained on how to become the White House Staff proper. All this was ordinarily in place to ensure an early transition. None of that had happened; there was no staff or team; so, Sybil knew she was starting off behind the eight ball. She was on her own for the moment. It was daunting.

However, the nation had not been created to fail; and the officers of the legislature, justice departments, the military, and the intelligence services all knew their roles and what the president had to know in order to perform her job as nearly seamlessly as possible.

Three minutes after the swearing-in ceremony, DNI Admiral David P. Jacobsen [Director of National Intelligence], Lt. Gen. Paul R. Reynolds the DIRNSA [Director of the National Security Agency], and the DCIA, knocked on the Oval Office door.

"Please come in," Sybil said, working herself up to be able to sound as if she were in charge—which, like it or not—she was.

"Madam President, I offer the congratulations of the entire seventeen intelligence services. It is a pleasure to have one of our own in the office again."

"Thank you, Director," she said and gave a friendly nod and smile to him and to her successor DCIA, Martin Obershauer.

"This will be an extraordinarily busy day for you, Madam President. I guess we should get started. This is the point when we share the nation's deepest secrets. I know that—as DCIA—you were privy to many secrets, but the president carried several more that even you didn't know about.

The presentation was Top Secret–eyes and ears only for the president–and was delivered in a monotone, emotionless, delivery despite the nearly incredible information Sybil was learning for the first time. Upon completion of the DNI's delivery, he turned the time over to the aide-de-camp, Army Major Jacob Marcussen to explain the "football".

"Madam President, what I am about to tell you and to show you is a matter of law, and it is Top-Secret. Not even everyone in this room is allowed to see the contents of this briefcase. The military aide carrying the "football" must remain physically close to the president at all times ready to carry out a well-rehearsed choreography of command and control. The options for nuclear war–called courses of action–vis a vis Russia, China, North Korea, etc., are contained in both the "Presidential Decision Handbook" which is handed off to each new, as well as in other more detailed briefings which will be refreshed from time to time and always at the time the president perceives the need to act.

"The so-called "football" is variously also known as the nuclear football, the atomic football, the president›s emergency satchel, the Presidential Emergency Satchel, the Button—even though there are no buttons—or sometimes, the Black Box, is in fact a briefcase—a rather heavy briefcase. I will show you and explain the contents of the president's emergency satchel, which are to be used by the President of the United States to authorize a nuclear attack while away from fixed command centers, such as the White House Situation Room. It is by–its nature and function–a mobile hub in the strategic defense system of the United States.

It is held by an aide-de-camp. Today, on this shift, that is me. There are a number of us; so many, that you may not be able to learn or to remember our names, even though our orders are that we be with you twenty-four hours a day, 365 days a year, and wherever you may be—even when you are in top-secret discussions. We all have the highest possible security ratings, entirely comparable to your own."

Major Marcussen opened the briefcase using a code that changed with each shift of aides-de-camp. There was a piece of paper containing directions for both the president and the aide-de-camp currently in control of the briefcase in a daily changing code regarding how to operate the machine inside using a separate complex code containing in the instruction paper.

"Note that there are computers, modems, radios, cell and satellite phones, even an instruction booklet, but no "button" as you can see. Our American nuclear weapons are launched by the highly secure communication of specified nuclear codes, nicknamed the "biscuit," which are changed daily. They authenticate the President's identity. Both the aide and the president have codes that need to be typed in separately to set the device into its terrible motion—launching a nuclear attack, perhaps even a holocaust."

The briefing was both daunting and sobering. President Norcroft-Daniels had just become the most powerful person in the world, having control of America's nuclear "triad" and more than 4,000 nuclear warheads around the world.

Under usual circumstances, the briefing traditionally takes place early on Inauguration Day and is conducted by the Strategic Command [the Omaha-based joint military command responsible for the strategic nuclear arsenal, and the White House Military Office]. Because this was anything but an ordinary inaugural day—and in the interest of time—the senior officers of the Strategic Command agreed to have Maj. Marcussen conduct the entire briefing and to do it in the Oval Office. He had spent the entire night in Omaha going over the strategic and tactical details of what would happen if a nuclear attack was considered to be necessary by the commander-in-chief. Marcussen was very bright and a quick learner; so, his recollection and presentation were flawless.

"Madam President, since the technical details and the day-to-day situations are so changeable, we should leave further details to the PDB [Presidential Daily Briefing presented as both a book and a verbal communication] for tomorrow at 0600."

She nodded gratefully. Her head was swimming already. Hopefully, she could get a night's rest to be able to be *compos mentis* enough to cope with another encyclopedia level set of information which was to come her way.

After the military, security, and intelligence, services completed their legally required transfer of information, it was the duty of the chief usher, Egan B. Caruthers, to convey to the new president succinct but critical information about moving in to assume control of the White House itself as well as the rest of the country.

"Madam President, if you feel you can trust me to take care of you and your family during this whirlwind transition process, I will give you a quick rundown and then I will take charge of seeing that things get done."

"Seems like a great idea to me, Egan," Sybil said, surprising the chief usher that she would know his name.

"All right, here is what will take place. First, I have to have a decision from you. How do you want the Oval Office to be decorated?"

"I don't have time to think about that. Leave it as it is, except for returning any personal items like photographs to the Willets family."

"Good. Then, the General Services Administration is directed by law to provide presidential transition services and facilities according to the GSA Act, including office space, equipment, and payment of certain related expenses to come from the Executive Office budgetary fund. Specifically, the act releases funding of approximately five million dollars, access to necessary government services, support for a transition team, and to provide training and orientation of new government personnel and other procedures to ensure an orderly transition.

"I hesitate to say it, but you, Ma'am, will have to begin delegating almost immediately to get a team together to form a new executive branch. You have no campaign staff, and it is the custom that all the previous administration's staffers and cabinet tender their resignations. You will need to make some critical decisions about that huge issue this very evening.

"I already have. Please convey to the Secretary of State that it is my wish that everyone in the White House remain in place and functioning as they did under President Willets for a time until I can get enough data to be able to make such weighty decisions."

"Consider it done, Madam President. And—if I may say so—I think that is a very wise decision on your part. Gives you some breathing room."

President Norcroft-Daniels nodded and gave him a smile acknowledging his willing loyalty and his desire to help get things going again.

"It will take a few days—even with all due haste being pursued—to get the additional personnel integrated into the preliminary daily operations and prepare them to take over the functions of government. I will have to deploy agency review teams, find experts to build out your initial management and policy agendas and schedule. I will round up a committee to work with you to identify key talent necessary to execute your priorities. I would hope that Congress and the foreign governments—even our enemies—will grant the customary 100-day honeymoon."

"Mr. Chief Usher, don't count on that, but it would be nice. However, I follow the gamblers creed: 'Trust everyone but always cut the cards yourself'."

He nodded, mindful of what this strong woman was going to be up against. It would be very interesting to see her history unfold. He crossed his fingers behind his back to wish her luck.

# CHAPTER TWO

Peace at last came at ten pm that first day of Sybil's presidency. Her husband, Charles, her daughter Cerisse, Cerisse's husband, Drake Farrer, and their two children, Lucia—age four—and Bonheur—age two— moved into the White House residence three hours before Sybil could finish her day and slowly shuffle into the living quarters. She felt numb with exhaustion, mental fatigue, and too much for one person to have absorbed in a single day—even for a woman with an IQ of 147. The rooms still smelled of fresh paint.

Cerisse and the children helped Sybil out of her shoes and confining business suit and herded her into the shower. The near scalding spray brought the new president back to life, and she threw on a silky robe.

Cerisse said, "Mom, we can only imagine what this day has been like. You can tell us sometime what you can. But now, you need to get some rest. Who knows what kind of calls you might get through the night?"

"You're right, my dear little daughter. I will obey your command; in fact, it would feel great not to be in command for a little while."

Charles took her hand and gently led her into their bedroom. She was very pleasantly surprised to see that the room appeared to be much like their bedroom at home in Georgetown had looked. The familiarity was comforting.

"How did all of this happen, my dear little husband?"

Charles was 6'4" tall and weighed 240 pounds. He worked out religiously and was a tightly muscled forty-five-year old Iron Man triathlete. He was a hunk, and Sybil found herself to be stirred—a condition she considered to be an impossibility after all the dignified problems she had handled during the day.

Charles put his arms around her, and after half an hour of massage, etc. the new president fell into deep below REM sleep feeling truly relaxed. Charles, and his massages, etc. always had that effect on her.

What she did not know is how much effort Charles and the family had put into getting the residence into ship-shape; so, that would be one less thing Sybil would have to be concerned about. The first family is responsible for getting all of their belongings to the White House themselves. Charles and the chief usher had supervised a coordinated effort with the government through private movers. Once the new president's belongings arrive, the residence staff takes custody of the possessions and begins unpacking. The chief usher gave considerable aid to Charles by coordinating move-in day which must take place with military precision. The process required–as is customary—500 people to ready the White House for the new administration and cannot commence until noon on inauguration day.

He gave Charles and the staff floor plans and photos to show where each item is to be placed. Because of the extra tight schedule Sybil was experiencing, they handled the logistical issues without even consulting the beleaguered new president. Usually, during the move-in process, the first family is together at the inauguration or watching the parade, then attending inaugural balls. This was different, and the staff had to work in high gear to get the rooms painted, re-carpeted, and the family belongings set in place. Usually, the process takes twelve hours; this time it took ten. The workman left the residence at ten to ten, just before their spies let them know that "Lioness" was on her way. That was the new secret service code for Sybil. She had a good laugh when she learned about it.

The next morning—day two—began with a jolt for Sybil. She was awakened at 0500 by her chief personal secret service guard. She was drowsy, out of sorts, and ready to snap at the intruder. Her grimace made him laugh despite the inappropriateness of the humor given that he was getting her up to prepare of the PDB [President's Daily Briefing]. The PDB is a vital part of this national security infrastructure. For the previous twenty-four hours the intelligence service had been working to prepare the book and summations of the nation's most sensitive intelligence reporting and analysis. For over fifty years, the U.S. intelligence community has delivered this top-secret book to the commander-in-chief every working day. Along with other support, the PDB helps the president remain the best-informed person on Earth on a wide range of global challenges.

The PDB began at exactly 0600 with introductions by the DNI. Next, the DCIA handed President Norcroft-Daniels the printed book. She knew from personal experience that the intelligence services had been up all night preparing it. The briefing was very detailed, compete, but succinct. No words or paragraphs wasted. There was one new troubling issue brought to the foreground.

"I wish the British thing would go away, Madam President," DCIA Obershauer said, "but it has not. You and the rest of us get along swimmingly with Lord Blancomb, the new PM; but, we cannot ignore the fact that the Brits attacked us, sank our ships, bombed our naval ship base in Norfolk, and killed some good Americans. We have talked with State, Defense, and our intelligence services. The world is holding its breath waiting to know if you are a hawk or a dove in the matter. There are hazards whatever you decide."

The president nodded, an indication that she would think about it and get back to them.

Immediately after the PDB, she buzzed her trusty secretary—actually President Willets trusty old secretary—to summon the secretaries of state, defense, homeland security, and the treasury to a meeting in the Green Room for brunch.

"Include the Speaker of the House, the Senate Majority Leader, and President Willet's Chief of Staff, Gen. Omar Zabriski."

"Copy," Mrs. Carpentier, the appointments secretary said crisply.

Sybil knew that Margarite Carpentier was the go-to person in Willets' White House—a veritable legend–and the veteran had been willing to stay on for the 100-day honeymoon period. She was adamant that it was her turn to have a life, and she and her family had plans. Plans that could not be cancelled or altered.

President Norcroft-Daniels spent most of the rest of day two working with committees to solve the hopelessly complicated and overwhelmingly time consuming requirement for her to read and hear brief descriptions of the important candidates for appointments, and listen to the recommendations put forward for 4,000 government positions, 1,000 of which required Senate confirmation— advise and consent, as per the Constitution.

The brunch was a proforma affair designed to meet-and-greet and to touch base with some of the most prickly personalities in the United States government. The brunch was good, the atmosphere, and the conversation convivial. It was held in the White House Mess, a small dining facility run by the Navy which is located in the basement of the West Wing next door to the Situation Room. The Mess could seat fifty people at a dozen tables. On this occasion, there was one table for the president's special brunch. The handsome wood table was adorned with elegant table White House embossed linens, fresh flowers, and official White House china. The room had a nautical ambience, decorated with wood paneling, nautical trim, and ship paintings.

On day three of Sybil Norcroft-Daniel's presidency, a somber meeting took place in the Cabinet Room.

Sybil took her seat at the oval mahogany conference table in the large West Wing room looking out onto the White House Rose Garden. The room adjoined the Oval Office–which was handy–otherwise the overwhelmingly busy new president might have established an unwanted precedent of tardiness during her first 100 days. A fireplace–flanked by two niches–was located on the north side of the room. Busts of George Washington and Benjamin Franklin by Jean-Antoine Houdon filled the niches. President Norcroft-Daniels had instructed the maintenance crew to light a fire in the fireplace to cut the cold of the day and to add a cheerful note to what promised to be a touchy meeting.

"Greetings, everyone. Thank you for meeting and for being prompt. I hardly need to tell you just how busy this week has been. First, let us observe a three-minute period of silence in honor of our dearly departed President Parker Conrad Willets. His will be a very difficult vacuum to fill."

The room was silent; some tears fell. But–after the meeting–the cabinet members commented to each other about how adroit the moment of silence gesture had been.

Sybil broke the silence, "My friends and fellow Americans, thank you all very much for staying on. We have a government to run, and the country needs to see us performing efficiently and successfully. Many of the things on your plates from a week ago will have to be postponed long enough to get the new administration up and going. My priorities are going to be summarized in a few requests—orders, actually.

I ask the secretaries of state, homeland security, treasury, and defense, to work with the intelligence services to prepare a report on the current status of the United Kingdom to assess two things: how much of the oligarchic influence still hangs over from Prime Minister Wood-Jackson's term, and how does that affect us? Second, I want an assessment of the economic and military capacity of the UK viz a viz payment of reparations to us for their phony war. That report needs to be final and on my desk before our next cabinet meeting next week.

"I want all the remaining secretaries to prepare documents of status of their departments and how costs can be curtailed, services improved, and efficiency enhanced. Report due next cabinet meeting. The week after, I want every department head to submit a secret memo to me listing the individuals in the country who might be considered for taking over for the present secretaries as time goes on. Tell me—for each choice—why you consider the man or woman to be desirable for the position. Again, on my desk by the start of next week's cabinet meeting."

Secretary of State Beverly Armont Willardson waited impatiently for the new president to finish talking.

"Madam President, it is the opinion of State, that we should let sleeping dogs in Europe lie. We have nothing to gain by going after them, and a great deal to lose.

"Plain as the nose on your face what you are after, no offense intended."

"None taken, but I still want the information in order to make intelligent decisions."

"All due deference, Madam President, but you are a novice at such things; you are not even a registered member of a political party. This should be handled with kid gloves and a nuanced approach; so, we don't upset our long-standing British friends or lose face in Europe by foolish moves."

"My order stands, Mr. Willardson. I will have the necessary intelligence data. Will you gather it or not?"

There was a pregnant pause. It was generally known that Willardson had little respect for the new president, had tangled with her before on the British question, and thought her to have been a poor choice to be vice president. He was on record on Wolf network, the far-right TV channel disparaging Sybil Norcroft-Daniels as a novice as a governmental figure and an upstart as president.

Sybil was quiet. Her eyes were blue ice as she engaged in a no-blink contest.

"No," Willardson said flatly holding Sybil's gaze defiantly.

"Is that your final decision?"

"It is. I believe you are off on a tangent by targeting the British, and nothing good can come of it. You are not ready to deal with the sophisticated Brits. They have several hundred years of experience on you, and they will eat your lunch."

Sybil turned to the Chief of Staff and whispered. He nodded and left the room.

"Secretary Willardson, thank you for your years of service to the nation and to the late President Willets. I respect you for having taken a firm position, but I must be able to pursue the course needed. Your resignation is in the top drawer of my desk. I accept it and wish you well. It will not be necessary for you to remain in this meeting any longer. Good day."

Then Willardson blinked.

The room was quiet for five minutes. Chief of Staff Gen. Zabriski walked back into the Cabinet Room followed by Rickard De Leon, the deputy chief of state for European affairs.

President Norcroft-Daniels whispered for a minute with Mr. De Leon, then had the steward lead him to the Secretary of State's recently vacated chair immediately to her right.

"Ladies and gentlemen, may I introduce the interim Secretary of State, Mr. Rickard De Leon, who has a long and distinguished career at state. I consider him to be eminently qualified for the position. He has agreed to head up the secret inquiry into UK matters.

"The next order of business is to find ways and means of getting at our crucial infrastructure problems. I have asked the chief of staff to head up a committee of cabinet secretaries, bipartisan congressional members, and important private citizens with experience and initiative. The secretaries of labor, commerce, treasury, and homeland security will be assigned areas of particular importance in this initiative. I expect a detailed and workable study and recommendations for commencement of projects by 100 days.

"Make this a maximum publicity, maximum public involvement, federal and state, program of collecting information; and Gen. Zabriski will give a summation of what has been learned and how to go forward.

"President Eisenhower's greatest enthusiasm and most important lasting legacy was the interstate highway system that most politicians said could not be done. We must get around, over, or through the nay-sayers and self-interested politicians and get this done. It will be a herculean task, and I am not yet even talking about the actual renovations and construction."

The next, and final, item on Sybil's agenda was to determine how to select a new—President Norcroft-Daniels'—cabinet, and how to find the right persons for the twenty-two positions not including—the president and vice-president, but including the chief of staff, the administrator of the EPA, the director of the OMB, administrator of the SBA, the chairperson of the Council of Economic Advisors, the ambassador of the United States Mission to the United Nations, and the ambassador of the United States Trade Representative—who were not customarily known by the citizenry to be holders of cabinet rank.

She requested that every cabinet member appoint a committee to make recommendations about who should replace him or her once the 100-day grace period was up. The cabinet members chuckled at the prospect of having to work themselves out of a job.

On day four, Sybil and Gen. Zabriski set aside two full hours for the most important meeting of the day. The new prime minister of the United Kingdom, Lord Blancomb, had responded immediately to President Norcroft-Daniel's request for an urgent meeting. He flew on a chartered British Airlines flight directly from Heathrow to Andrews AFB and arrived five minutes before the appointed hour for his meeting.

Mrs. Carpentier announced his presence to the occupants of the Oval office—the president, chief of staff, secretaries of defense, state, homeland security, and the CJCS.

Sybil got up from behind her desk, walked briskly to the door, extended her hand and ushered the pm warmly into the gathering.

# CHAPTER THREE

It was hardly necessary; but for the sake of etiquette and to set a tone of formality, Sybil made introductions all around. Lord Blancomb was uncomfortable with the formality because he and wanted and expected to have more-or-less a one-on-one heart-to-heart with his friend, Sybil.

The president said, "Mr. Prime Minister, everyone in this room knows what a great service and act of selfless courage you made to save our two countries from a foolish and futile war. I repeat my promise to you that no one else knows about what you did other than the two CIA agents you worked with are aware. In my capacity as president of the United States and on behalf of all Americans, I thank you."

She gave the prime minister a small bow to punctuate her sincerity.

"I acted out of concern for my own country. Our recently retired despot would have plunged us into a conflict from which there could be no return for us. Besides, I like the US," he replied with a friendly smile. "It was time posthumous, for him to go. Napoleon is credited with saying—before he made himself emperor—'Ambition is never content, even at the summit of greatness'."

"Lord Blancomb, I need to make reference to a certain numbered account in the Caribbean of which you are well aware. Its existence is a state secret and no one outside this room is aware of it. Its usefulness has come to an end, I am sure you realize. The money is yours—yours personally–and there is no need for any of it to return to us."

The PM interrupted, "But, Madam President, I never for a moment considered keeping the money. I accepted it in the way I did in order to be convincing to your agents that I was sincere, as strange as that may seem. I have an extensive espionage experience, and you and I know that it is safer to trust an asset who is venal enough to do it for money than a budding hero who does it for emotional or ideological reasons. I have the number for the account in my pocket, and I intend to turn it over to you for return to the proper US accounts."

"That is good of you but leave it alone for the moment. Unfortunately, I and all the officers of the United States government gathered here today, are caught on the horns of a dilemma. Our quandary rests on a decision we must make. How to deal with Great Britain? Under your despotic–but duly elected predecessor–lethal and very costly attacks were made by your armed forces and intelligence services. Attacks were carried out on our soil, against our ships, and to the lethal suffering of our people. I did not ask you here to chastise you. Indeed, I praise you for what you have done to restore order and decency in the United Kingdom. It will take time—considerable time—for you to restore your honor, your credibility, and your place beside us in councils of war, trade, diplomacy, and as trusted allies."

"I realize all of that, of course. I can only pledge my uttermost to mend that which was broken by us. And, yes, it will take time. I implore you–as officers of the United States–to trust my word and my pledge."

"Once our ships took the first hit, and our people lost their first sons and daughters, the climate turned dark. It will take more than apologies and pledges, I'm afraid. There is serious debate, even now, about whether or not to conduct attacks on Great Britain to inflict damage and injury comparable to that we sustained—no asymmetric level of intensity. No one is suggesting that we do anything more to you than was done to us.

"On the other side of the argument, there are those who call attention to our long friendship and history of mutual assistance as allies. Those people suggest that we forgive and forget. Frankly, I think the nation is about evenly divided. I am in a damned if I do and damned if I don't position. It is a general rule of politics never to commit oneself for a cause that fifty percent of the voters oppose.

"To my mind, there is a possible compromise; no one gets everything they want; but everyone comes to believe that their argument was at least heard; and there is some measure of justice that has occurred."

"I beg your pardon, Madam President, but what compromise can there be to this conundrum?"

"I'm glad you asked. The only way I can see is for the UK to make restitution in so far as that is possible, and reparations to bring about some sort of closure to the families of the killed and injured."

"I hate to appear to grovel, Madam President; but our previous prime minister and his avaricious populist cronies effectively looted the treasury, threw away any friendships that might stand us in good stead from whom we can borrow. I am in the position of being the beggar at the feast—a guilty beggar at that."

"Not you, Sir...your country. I tell you in all candor that you must do something. Take a week and confer with your government, your citizens, and your officers about what can be done. I repeat, nothing is not an answer."

"A week?!" Lord Blancomb said in dismay.

"That is enough. It is not like this is breaking news. And it is not like there have not been discussions. I am sure that there are still Britains of good conscience who seek to do the right thing. Please get back to me with a proposal, My Lord. Our people are not in a particularly forgiving mood just now."

The British prime minister was disconsolate, and he carried that mood back with him to the halls of parliament and the offices of the leaders of the commonwealth.

The fifth day was dedicated to the pressing issue of the condition of the infrastructure of the United States.

President Norcroft-Daniels was determined to get the repairs underway as quickly as possible and to make the issue the most crucial for her administration and for her legacy.

Fifty people gathered in the White House China Room which is located near the Map Room on the Residence's ground floor. They sat on uncomfortable folding chairs, and each attendee had a pen and spiral notebook for taking their own notes. The president did not allow simple refreshments, not even a bottle of water. She was determined that, at least, the rudiments of a plan would emerge.

No one seemed to mind, especially the selected people who came of their own volition, at their own expense, and with determination to see to it that bipartisan, American—not political results—were accomplished.

President Norcroft-Daniels introduced herself to the assemblage, many of whom had scarcely ever heard of her. Many of them knew her only dimly as having recently been appointed to the vice-presidency. Reporters were present and allowed every freedom to record the proceedings; but, since it was not a political or propaganda affair, they were not allowed to ask questions except during the infrequent breaks.

"My fellow-Americans, we come here from all walks of life with the determination to get a crucial job done for our country. Most of you are volunteers, but have been carefully selected because of your knowledge, experience, expertise, willingness to work. Make no mistake, I am asking you to work, to sacrifice, and to stand up for what you believe must be accomplished. We have a few politicians..."

There were a few light-hearted boos.

"... lawyers..."

Even more boos and some laughing.

"...miners, construction leaders, labor leaders, doctors and nurses, administrators, road builders, HVAC and plumbing experts, bridge repair crewmen, water services engineers, and plenty of other engineers. Everyone here is a builder or a repair person in one way or other. We are not necessarily proposing large scale new construction, just that we get our present infrastructure back to a level of acceptable safety, efficiency, and accountability. We must get to the level of this year PDQ, and then get on with planning and preparing for the future. We need to have a country of which we can be proud—clean, safe, efficient, and a pleasure to be in. We must have clean water, clean air, clean streets, well-handled sewage systems, water systems, airports, highways, and so on and so on. So, roll up your sleeves, and let's get to work."

There was hearty applause, but a measured concern about how much of this extraordinarily ambitious mission could be accomplished in practicality.

The next—and concluding speaker—was Neal Dastrup, PhD.

"Ladies and gentlemen, this is the first in a series of lectures I have been asked to give by the president on the needs of the American infrastructure. This will be an overview of the problem areas: Let's start with bridges. Everyone here is aware of the sudden collapse of the I-35 West bridge near down-town Minneapolis, Minnesota in

2007 which dropped the middle portion of the bridge more than 100 feet into the Mississippi river. Thirteen people were killed, 145 injured; and a very important artery of the Interstate was severed disrupting transportation and commerce for more than a year. Repairs cost more than $300 million.

"There are more than 600,000 US bridges; on average they are 56 years old; and many of them are more than 60 years old. Engineers from the American Road and Transportation Builders Association have studied most of the bridges and have declared that 54,000 are in need of repair right now. 465 of those bridges are similar in design to the I-35W span, and it is accurate to say that all of them need to be repaired and reinforced.

"Detailed inspection and reinforcement of all these bridges are vitally important as the nation begins to think about upgrading its infrastructure. The I-35W and similar spans are not isolated cases but instead, as harbingers of a problem that plagues much infrastructure and development of the last 60 years—more than just bridges. The problem for bridges mainly is what engineers call 'fracture-critical' design.

"Bridges across the United States are deteriorating. The expected lifespan for an American bridge is only 50 years. As of this date, the average age of an American bridge is 42 years. Nine percent of them are structurally deficient. The ARTBA [American Road and Transportation Builders Association], produced a more recent report that estimates it will take more than 80 years to fix all of them.

Eighty years!, and we have hardly even started. More than 47,000 bridges in the United States are in imminent danger and are in crucial need of repairs. Economic decisions by the previous administration resulted in the pace of repair slowing to its lowest point in five years.

"$70.9 billion is needed to address the current backlog of deficient bridges. In sum, America's infrastructure is desperately in need of investment, according to the American Society of Civil Engineers. The ASCE estimates the US needs to spend some $4.5 trillion by 2025 to fix the country's roads, bridges, dams, airports, schools, and other infrastructure. The American Society of Civil Engineers' 2017 Infrastructure Report Card–published every four years—gives US infrastructure a D+ grade.

"We will have to deal with bridges in more depth in the days to come; but, in the interests of time, we need to go on to list the problems of America's infrastructure, at least. The infrastructure is more than just a network of roads, bridges, tunnels, ports, railroads and airports connecting our towns, cities and states, of course. It serves as a backbone of economic growth and preserves our safety, quality of life, and prosperity. The United States has long been a global leader in innovation, transportation and smart fiscal policies, yet the infrastructure that keeps our country open for business is now far out of date and puts us in danger.

"During the 1930s, 4.2 percent of our country's GDP was spent on infrastructure investment; but by 2016, that number fell to 1.5 percent and is going further down each year. According to the Brookings Institute, between 2007 and 2017, total public spending on infrastructure fell by $9.9 billion in real terms, taking into consideration inflation. There always seems to be something more important for our federal and state governments to hold their attention. And–heaven forbid, that we even think about raising taxes; that is the political third rail.

"In short, our nation's infrastructure is crumbling, and we need real, sustainable investment; and we need it yesterday. The American Association of Civil Engineers estimated—based on grades of the quality of 16 categories of infrastructure every four years–that the nation's roads, dams, airports and water and electrical systems need $4.6 trillion of work–more than the entire federal government spends in a year. The subject of what to do about correcting our flawed infrastructure will have to wait for another day. But, bear in mind that all of you have been charged with finding workable solutions.

"Today, we have taken a quickie view of bridges. For the rest of this session, we will consider the condition of roads, schools, airports and air traffic control systems and projects that the FAA has thus far excluded–such as parking facilities and airplane hangars, water treatment plants, sewage systems, pipelines, energy plants, other physical assets, and operation and maintenance."

For the remainder of the long afternoon, Dr. Dastrup presented a succinct summary of the needs of the sixteen critical infrastructure sectors of the United States:

- Chemical Sector
- Commercial Facilities Sector

- Communications Sector.
- Critical Manufacturing Sector
- Dams Sector
- Defense Industrial Base Sector
- Emergency Services Sector
- Energy Sector
- Financial Services Sector
- Food and Agriculture Sector
- Government Facilities Sector
- Healthcare and Public Health Sector
- Information Technology Sector
- Nuclear Reactors, Materials, and Waste Sector
- Transportation Systems Sector
- Water and Wastewater Systems Sector

When Dr. Dastrup concluded, the president gave the volunteers a final sobering message to think about and to wrestle with.

"Finally, my friends, always bear in mind that everyone involved in the questions of how to deal with infrastructure issues has an agenda. Unions want jobs for their members. Engineers want to contribute unique, aesthetic, and costly designs to provide careers for their members; the engineers' society spent $12 million lobbying in Washington since 1999. Hospitals, big pharma, and providers' associations, want more and better for their members. The airports council spent $23 million on lobbying during that same period. The National Association of Manufacturers recently released a report calling for $1.3 trillion more to be spent over 10 years on transportation infrastructure. Do you suppose that all of that comes from altruism?

"Among just a few groups who have petitioned, or which have written letters, or testified before Congress are such diverse groups as: the U.S. Chamber of Commerce, the AFL-CIO, FedEx, the American Water Works Association, and BMW of North America. Beware of the wolves in sheep's clothing.

"The engineers society tells us that roads and bridges need $2 trillion in improvements. The Federal Highway Administration says they need $836 billion. The engineers' society estimates that drinking-water systems need $1 trillion over 25 years to maintain and expand service, but the Environmental Protection Agency says they need $384 billion or less. The same engineers' society says the 15,000 dams most in need of rehabilitation require $45 billion of rebuilding. The Association of State Dam Officials puts the price at less than half that. Who should we believe? My friends, you have some thorny issues to deal with, and puzzles to put aright, and knots to untie. I know that what I ask of you is most difficult; but, I also know that you are Americans. Like the motto of the SeaBees, we "can do."

# CHAPTER FOUR

The sixth day of Sybil Norcroft Daniels' presidency started well. The PDB revealing little that was new other than the economic hardship being suffered by Iranians was increasing and was associated with sporadic riots against the government. The IRI [Islamic Republic of Iran government] castigated the United States because of its harsh economic sanctions and made numerous threats of retaliation—up to and including a nuclear strike. The CIA continued to report that Iran did not have nuclear weapon capability. A new issue–coming from the FBI and the CIA–was that some problems appeared to be developing on two racial fronts: unemployment and accusations of police profiling and brutality against African-Americans in multiple large cities, and a sharp increase in the number and intensity of activity by white supremacist and nativist organizations. The impression was that none of those problems had reached an actionable level.

President Daniels had her secretaries clear her appointment schedule sufficiently enough to allow her adequate time to prepare for her first televised speech to the nation and to meet with the committee to find a new vice-president.

She had typed in just three preliminary words for her speech to begin the rough draft of suggestions she wanted her speech writers to consider, when, at 10:06, her red phone rang.

"What is it?" she asked Mrs. Carpentier, her secretary who was a holdover from the Willets administration.

"Trouble."

"What kind of trouble?"

"The FBI kind. He's on the line, and he says its both important and urgent."

Sybil did not have to ask who "he" was. It could be none other than the DFBI Landon Murphy.

"What's up, Landon?"

"Thirty minutes ago, two police officers serving an eviction notice were gunned down and their bodies mutilated by a large crowd of young men and women in the Red Hook neighborhood of northwestern Brooklyn. Are you familiar with it, Madam President?"

"Thoroughly. What evidence is available about the actions of the perpetrators and of the police?"

"We have maybe three dozen cell phone videos of the actions. Our experts are sure that the videos have been doctored to show only police responding. That is, the first parts of every video have been removed to get rid of the original violence."

"You say, 'we'. Why is the FBI involved?"

"NYPD intelligence division is gathering considerable evidence that a highly organized and violent civil disobedience plan is about ready to be unleashed on the city. The commissioner called me and asked for federal help. We agreed to help, but from here on, the 'buck stops at your desk' to gerrymander an old phrase of Harry Truman's."

"What actions have already been taken?"

"NYPD first and foremost right now wants to retrieve their comrades' bodies. Then, the commissioner is going to send in a small army to cordon off a ten-block area surrounding the crime scene–The Red Hook Houses–two connected public housing complexes managed by the NYCHA [New York City Housing Authority]. It is the largest housing development in Brooklyn and probably the most dangerous."

"What are your plans, Landon?"

"Help NYPD wherever and whenever we can. We plan to keep our footprint small and obscure to start with."

"Good, keep me posted. We do not want this to escalate to a major race war or blacks versus cops war. I was in LA during the riots in April, 1992. On the twenty-ninth, anger boiled over after four LAPD officers were found not guilty of assaulting Rodney King, leading to several days of widespread and massive violence. The chant was, 'burn, baby, burn'. Do you remember that, Landon?"

"Vividly. And I remember that the LAPD pretty much let them burn down their own neighborhoods and concentrated on saving the surrounding, more affluent...more white...neighborhoods. What a colossal mess!"

"I am determined that we won't see a repeat on my watch."

"I am too, of course, Madam President. That's why we are beefing up the city's riot gear and weaponry. In LA they had too little and too late. We and the good cops are going to be prepared this go around."

"And we are all going to do our best not to see another Ferguson, Missouri debacle. I was there, too. A series of several protests which degenerated into riots. The whole thing was set on a backdrop of severe and mounting African-American unrest. The final spark that blew up the powder keg was the protest triggered by the fatal shooting of Michael Brown, an 18-year-old African American, by Darren Wilson, a white police officer, on August 9th, 2014."

"No winners there, as I recall. No real improvement or joy since, Ma'am."

"All too true. I repeat; keep me posted as frequently as necessary, Landon. We must not let this get out of hand."

As soon as the DFBI left the line, Sybil had a call but through to her friend, former CIA special agent, Dominic D'Orio, who was currently chief of intelligence for the NYPD.

"This is a secure line," the White House operator said. "I have a call from the president of the United States for Captain Dominic D'Orio."

"Yes, Ma'am, I will get him immediately."

"D'Orio speaking," the police captain said.

"Dominic, do you recognize my voice? I would rather keep our conversation and relationship on the down-low."

"Sure. Congratulations anyway. Are you settled in?"

"Not hardly. Too many big things to worry about. How bad is this Red Hook thing?"

"On the surface, it would seem like a riled-up neighborhood misunderstanding the facts and wanting to blame the cops. That comes with the job. But, underneath, my guys think it's orchestrated. There has been an influx of several gang leaders who usually would as soon kill each other as talk. We have CIs and some cops who are undercover and are getting the straight skinny about what's going on. The killing of the two cops was a planned caper. The gangstas rounded up guys and quite a few women bangers to be there, take pictures, and to create chaos to obscure the identities of the murderers.

"Talk around Red Hook is that a big march is planned which will end in a big riot. The NYPD and the NYFD are sitting in their trucks ready to roll; but, Madam President, tensions are building. Yes, there's fighting mad ghetto people; but there are cops who are ready to shoot on site. There's a lot of fed-up guys in blue who think the citizens are being coddled by the politicians and being fired-up by the bangers to get revenge for what happened. The cops are talking pre-emptive strike and bringing in the big guns, even a couple of the surplus tanks left over from the War in Iraq. I think it will be time to bring in the national guard sooner instead of later."

"You think it's that bad now?"

"Better to prevent than to try and cure later."

"Speaking of politicians, what is your take on what Mayor Jones wants and what will he do?"

"He'll listen to you, but he is of the highly melanotic hue; and he comes from Brownsville and gets prickly when Brooklyn, especially north and east Brooklyn get criticized. He was put into office by his people, and he is ready to go fang and claw at anyone who challenges them. He is constantly at loggerheads with the NYPD. Unfortunately, the neighborhood is one of the few Brooklyn neighborhoods that have not seen signs of gentrification; and Mayor Jones is frustrated by the slow pace of improvement there.

"He considers it to be 'Whitey's' fault. The neighborhood is filled with public housing for lower income residents. Brownsville has had the highest poverty level and crime rate in New York City for as long as anybody can remember. No cop says out loud that it is the 'murder capital of New York', but it is. The mayor would like nothing better than to make you look like a fool. I think it would be better to send a lower ranked African-American to have a *tête-à-tête*. Once you go to talk to him, he knows that he has talked to *numero uno*, and there is no higher authority. He can consider that a great win. He is ambitious."

"That's a lot to chew on, Dominic. Thanks for the candor. I will do my best to see peace in Brooklyn...with your help."

Sybil's next call was to Walt Bennett, governor of New York.

When he came on the line, she said, "Walt, congratulations on the big win in New York this cycle. We are both learning that trouble goes down the funnel to us once we get into such positions. Do you need our help for this Red Hook thing?"

"Not obviously right now. But, my gut, and my operatives, tell me that the lid is going to blow off soon. Professional agitators are all over in the city. The citizens of Red Hook are getting the message via the grapevine to start hoarding essentials...including weapons of all kinds. There some complaints that service stations are running out of gas. Every vehicle in that 'hood must have a full tank ready to serve the cause'."

"I'll back you completely when you call out the national guard, but I want caution. Don't have it be the cops or the soldiers who fire the first round. Have your photographers everywhere; so, we can have at least a chance at getting the truth once the fire-breathers calm down. Anything else we can do to help?"

"Maybe, and maybe now is the time. I think it would do a lot of good for you and for me to have a round of talks with the people in the neighborhoods—try to convince them not to burn down the town."

"There's a lot of wisdom in that. I'll send a few sensible people to New York to try and set up neighborhood coffee klatches between the appropriate police people and the law-abiding grandmothers and people with jobs and maybe some education who can listen to reason."

"Send them and General Harkinsson from the guard to my office first. Let's coordinate from there."

"I agree. I am of the opinion that the presence of feds should be kept as much out of the limelight as possible. I hope this can be seen as local and not some war between Red Hook and Brownsville people and the U.S. government."

"Nice talking to you, Madam President. And, I return the congratulations. You probably feel a bit overwhelmed at this point less than a week into your presidency. You seem to be handling things well. It goes a long way further with me to have a talk than to be dictated to."

"Same with me. Let's remember that as things progress."

Sybil's communication with the senior officers of the New York National Guard was smooth and quick. She guaranteed help and support from the federal government and a noninterference policy. She joked that she was "here from the government, and I came to help."

She and the general and his two colonels hashed out the rough draft of a plan. Every precaution had to be in place before she went to New York to attempt to converse with the locals about how close to the brink they all were.

The new president was back in her office to deliver her first address to the nation as president.

The director raised his right hand showing five fingers pointing up, "Five, four, three, two, one," and he pointed at the president's mouth.

"My fellow Americans, this is my first time to speak to you as your president. I mourn the untimely death of my predecessor, President Willets. I had the privilege and pleasure of working for the man and admired him. I regret his loss as our president, as our wise leader, and as my personal friend.

"As a nation, we face real challenges from within and without. Iran and North Korea remain unwilling to join the family of nations. The Russians and sometimes the Chinese aid and abet those rogue nations. We are still actively engaged in a low level of combat with the Syrian regime and their Russian and Islamic State enablers. However, presently, the lid is still on that pot. I will undoubtedly have to speak to you further as changes may dictate.

"Our infrastructure is in deplorable condition, and a small army of volunteer workers and exports have agreed to my plea to come up with an affordable solution, presumably a long-term effort. Often in the past, other expenditures have outweighed the repair and maintenance effort; but this time, there seems to be a respite from other costly necessities. Mark my words; repair of the infrastructure will be costly; probably, a trillion dollars or there abouts. That is trillion with a "T".

"We have smoldering tensions on racial, political, ideological, and religious lines. They threaten to become violent occasionally. We are prepared to deal with that. However, please hear my plea; learn to talk to each other, even if your views differ. We are Americans, for heaven's sake. Let us all act like it. Build; don't tear down. Help, don't hinder. We are all in this together.

"I will conclude on a sobering note. We must hang together. There are several individuals and groups who are talking secession. I say that will happen only over my dead body. Right now, there are people acting contrary to all that is needed by America to push racial divisions over the brink. Know this, we will have law and order; we will achieve civility in discourse; and we will keep America the most powerful, the best moral example, and the home of equality and freedom. God bless America and all her people. Pray for me."

# CHAPTER FIVE

**D**ay seven started with a bang, a literal bang. President Daniels was awakened by her secret service guard at 0215—O dark thirty—as her husband Charles described it. She was rushed to the Situation Room where the bank of television sets showed what looked—a first glance—like a Fourth of July celebration on steroids, and all over the country.

"Madam President, this all started within fifteen minutes ago. Explosions, firebombs, arsonists, and looters, came out of the woodwork at precisely the same time in DC, New York, Chicago, Salt Lake City, and Los Angeles. That's just so far; I have to guess that we'll see more of it later tonight," Landon Murphy reported.

"We have national guards up and ready in every one of those states. The cops and firefighters are overwhelmed and are in retreat. We await your orders," General Glen Gabler, Sr., the CJCS said.

Sybil did not hesitate, "Mobilize the national guards in every state with a large ghetto population. Tell the state generals that we hope to see a definite presence just outside the ghettos or any other hot spot. Let's not start shooting just yet. We'll follow the lead of the locals about entering the center cities or becoming part of the violence. However, I have a personal and now a national policy of not allowing American first responders or armed forces to have to take fire without returning it. Measured response is fine sometimes, but I think it is time to react more like the Israelis—sevenfold."

"Aye, aye, Madam President," the CNO said.

"Copy," said Gen. Gabler.

And the action and reaction were set into motion.

More televisions became scenes of glowing fire and mass destruction as Seattle, San Diego, Denver, and Omaha, lit up. Police were absolutely overwhelmed and made orderly retreats to the suburbs. Fire fighters and EMS units finally refused to become human torches and moved miles from the holocaust taking place. Compton, California became a looters' heaven with no police or security forces to interrupt the looters. Ogden, Utah's East Central neighborhood became so unmanageable that the city's law enforcement moved out and watched in frustration as generally law-abiding citizens became looting marauders.

"Dallas, Texas has a generally poor reputation so far as violent crime is concerned, but on this day, every police officer in the surrounding cities gathered for a unified march to be able to save hospitals, patients, and several nursing homes, from massacres. Five Points—one of Dallas's highest populated neighborhoods–exploded in murder, mayhem, pedestrian deaths, and fire, starting from an epicenter where Route 352 and Scyene Road met, despite a police task force already in place from a month earlier. Another of Dallas's most violent neighborhoods—the Ross-Bennet Grid–followed suit. Flagrant robberies, street drug sales, and violence, seemed to affect every street and building. Almost at the exact same time, the Forest-Audalia Grid made its television debut.

The president watched with mounting fury and pity as city after city descended into hellfire and her aspirations to make a better America turn to ashes.

"Move the national guard units into everywhere there is a riot or a car fire, or an attack on police. Use some discretion, like rubber bullets; but get law and order. If those police and national guard units cannot gain control within a day, I will order a national state of martial law which will allow us to bring in the armed forces of the United States. That has only happened once so far as I know. It happened in San Diego, California, and was quite successful, so far as I know."

The attorney general asked, "Madam President, are you sure you have the right to make such orders?"

"I am. I have been studying the question since I first learned that we should expect this kind of disorder. I am going to go ahead, but it wouldn't hurt to put some of the dozens of White House attorneys to work. Would you head up that project, General?"

"I still wonder if you shouldn't wait a bit. You have enemies; every president does. They could look to this as grounds for impeachment."

"Well, I guess this is why I get paid the big bucks. It is on me, and I am not going to allow this anarchy to go on. This I know from my cursory check on the laws. The president has the authority to declare a national emergency and have any or all of the state governors declare state emergencies and to request Marines, and any other federal troops be brought in—I can use any and all federal military forces in domestic peace keeping missions to enforce federal laws, quell insurrection, and keep the peace. Check out the U.S. Constitution, the 1807 Act, and the Posse Comitatus Act of 1878. They all state unequivocally that the President retains command of these forces under his or her duties as commander-in-chief during their domestic use. Now, forgive me, General, I have work to get done. We'll have to worry about impeachment another day."

He shrugged, not entirely convinced; but, she apparently had the *cohones* [Spanish for courage] to push her decision forward, whatever the personal cost.

Sybil was not immune to the gravity of what she had ordered; but she was in the right; and she would defend herself when necessary—some other day.

For the next three days, the president and her military officers, and several major urban police chiefs lived in the Situation Room. The White House chefs brought in three meals a day, and the chief usher even had cots brought in. As the Godfather would say when he went to war with his rival mafia chieftains, "We're going to the mattresses."

The United States military had put into place rapid response plans since the LAPD requested federal help during the riots in 1992 and the Twin Towers bombings in 2001.

Information poured in from all over the country. A dozen officers worked full time to analyze and collate the streams of bad news. The Deputy CJCS reported to President Daniels every hour at least. The federal, state, and local enforcement, officials had the plan well in mind and the resources to carry out her orders. Sybil's problem was to keep self-control enough to resist the urge to micromanage the tactical actions on the ground. She had set in motion the strategic orders; now, she had to suffer the pangs of frustration brought on by waiting.

The early reports the first day were grim. Apparently, the rioters had effectively convinced the citizens of the ghettos that the fault lay with the various governments and that the organizers of the riots were not only in the right, but they had a good plan to bring the president and the governors to heel. Hour after hour the TVs lit up with more fires and the echoes of past chanting of "Burn, baby, burn!" What was less apparent to any civilian viewer of the television networks were the inexorable advances of the well-coordinated law enforcement and military forces.

The first encounter of police backed up by marines took place in Chicago's Chatham neighborhood. Chatham–of Chicago's 76 neighborhoods—was the most dangerous. The watchers in the Situation Room followed the vest cam videos of four police officers responding to a mob-violence scene. They moved into the area located between 79th and 93rd street along route 90/94 at speed, headed towards the location given by CPD dispatchers. There was conversation among the officers and the marines that this could be a trap.

They arrived at the scene in time to save an old man, his wife, and two grandchildren, from being killed by the inflamed mob. The mobsters were well armed and not about to back down to any authority.

CPD sergeant Mark O'Brien shouted through a bull horn, "CPD. Put down your weapons. You are all under arrest. Put down your weapons and disperse, or we will arrest you for inciting a riot, aggravated assault, and conspiracy to commit murder!"

O'Brien's orders fell on deaf ears. The mobsters sneered in arrogant defiance. There were several onlookers taking iPhone videos. But this time, the police had their own videographers to catch the whole escalating criminal activity.

O'Brien quietly told his fellow police officers to advance slowly behind shields. A few of the criminals began to edge away and to leave down side streets. A very few put down their weapons as the phalanx of police officers came closer, backed up by marines in armored personnel carriers, heavy machine guns at the ready.

The terrorized family huddled together on the sidewalk.

There were about a dozen remaining gangstas, all of them fingering the triggers of their AK-47s and machine pistols, more defiant than ever.

CPD sergeant O'Brien shouted back to marine lieutenant Glade Turnigan, "Cover us, Lieutenant."

Turnigan gave his men orders. Marines stood on their vehicles, assumed combat firing positions, and chambered rounds.

"Go," Turnigan ordered, and the marines opened fire on the astonished, then quickly dead gang of thugs.

"Cease fire."

O'Brien looked almost as astonished as the gang members, "I ask you to cover us, what was all of that?"

Turnigan replied laconically, "That's what marines do when covering fellow fighters."

Viewing the action from inside the Situation Room, General Gabler, said, "I think we have a failure to communicate. Cops take the request to provide cover as to remain at the ready and behind the advancing officers. Marines take the request to mean 'provide covering fire to fellow combatants heading into imminent danger.' We'll have to get boots on the ground to give a few lessons on the difference between civilian cop lingo, and the way trigger ready marines, soldiers, and SEALs understand things."

President Daniels gritted her teeth and counted herself and the military lucky that no marines or cops had been injured or killed. In fact—thus far—the only casualties were the two original police officers who were murdered during the night.

At nightfall, the glow of the city fires was all the more vivid, indicative that the rioting was far from being under control. The only real success was achieved by the DC Metro police and a large unit of the Maryland National Guard who surrounded the capitol, the White House, and the Supreme Court building. That made the efforts of the assailants impotent, and DC appeared to have entered into a disquieting calm–but a calm–which was encouraging to everyone in the Situation Room.

By morning–around the country–there were fewer new fires and the fire departments backed up by police and National Guardsmen were beginning to be able to fight some of them. There were still new fires starting sporadically. Several thousand rioters had been arrested and herded into hastily made internment centers to be booked and processed. Jails and prisons were rapidly becoming unable to accommodate more guests.

The rioters had been well trained on how to keep their traitorous attacks underway by employing guerrilla methods.

President Daniels had General Hoyt C. Oldroyd, head of the USCINCSOC [Commander in Chief, U.S. Special Operations Command], brought to the Situation Room.

"General Oldroyd, thanks for getting here so quickly. I know you are aware of the changing tactics on the part of the rioters. I need you to organize your command into units—lots of units—to move into the inner cities on capture or kill missions. For the record–if in question–the men and women in your units are ordered to protect themselves and innocent civilians above all else. No police officer or soldier has been shot or killed…yet…and I want that admirable record to continue. Sir, I am depending on you and your black ops people to make a dramatic change in this war that has reached something of a static state. We need to convince the rioters that their enterprise is futile and too costly to continue. Any questions?"

"Only one, Madam President, do I have carte blanche to carry out your orders?"

"Within the rules of war and this engagement, yes. Report back to the Situation Room as frequently as feasible."

"Copy that," General Oldroyd said and snapped to attention with a crisp salute.

# CHAPTER SIX

Undercover FBI, NSA, MISO [Military Information Support Operations] and metropolitan police department agents, shared information on a grand scale to the JTF [temporary Joint Task Force] under the leadership of Lieutenant General Evan S. Celementia, commander of the 1ˢᵗ Infantry Division from Fort Riley, Kansas. At the president's orders, the JTF took command of all federal, state, and local, military forces.

The FBI became the de facto lead civilian police force. The third day of widespread conflict in the country looked very much like the first two days—a destructive stalemate. The main difference on day three was that an unprecedented mountain of data was collected and was transmitted by computer to the JTF HQ [temporarily part of Air Force Global Strike Command Strategic Air Command (SAC) was both a United States Department of Defense (DoD) Specified Command and a United States Air Force (USAF) Major Command (MAJCOM)], located on Marine Corps Base Quantico, Virginia. Every asset of the US Armed forces was turned to that JTF base of operations.

The CIA assisted the DOD intelligence services to sift out the most crucial information, and to plan for tactical operations. The air force readied its fighters and helicopter services to assist as necessary in the direct commando missions and to ferry fighters to the many hot spots around the country.

General Hoyt C. Oldroyd's, U.S. Special Operations Command was given information pertinent to the location and activities of every major city's worst perpetrators. Gen. Oldroyd's staff assembled the special ops forces and gave them specific assignments. In all cases, the missions were to capture or eliminate the "WOW"'s [worst of the worst] hiding places and the locations of their planned future attacks. They were dispatched as rapidly as they could be fully armed, informed of their missions, and loaded on planes. The first began arriving in Washington DC and New York City at 0600, and the last unit out left Quantico for Los Angeles at 1700 EST.

Real time reports began to filter in at 0645, then came rapidly and frequently thereafter.

At 0645, the Washington DC FBI Office at 555 11th Street Northwest, and the office located at 601 4th Street Northwest, reported that special agents from their two locations accompanied forty Special Operations specialists to presumed empty warehouses in the city were they engaged heavily armed and fully resisting gang fighters. It appeared that the fight would become a stalemate even though the Special Agents and the Special Operations specialists killed or critically wounded fifteen gangstas. Information gleaned from adroit questioning of the wounded revealed that the warehouse contained tons of flame throwers, incendiary bombs, thermite canisters, and napalm. The lieutenant in charge of the Special Ops group called in an air strike from nearby Joint Base Anacostia-Bolling. The building and its occupants were reduced to fine ash seven minutes later. It was estimated that more than a hundred hostiles were killed, and seventeen tons of flammable weapons and ammunition were destroyed.

There was quiet and hopeful applause when the report came into the Situation Room at 0710.

Shortly after the reports began to come to the Situation Room about DC, the black-ops mission in Red Hook, Brooklyn preliminary reports began to filter in, complete with videotapes. Under cover of semi-darkness, and with the rioters either sleeping off drug or alcohol induced stupors and the occasional new fire starting up, the NYPD intelligence officers led a detachment of twenty-two army CAG [Combat Applications Group Delta Force elite counter-terrorism experts] to the south block of the Red Hook Houses government projects. The intelligence officers and a SWAT unit provided back-up cover—the kind of cover where a reserve unit helps protect the forward unit without immediately commencing heavy fire.

The SOF (Special Ops Forces) each carried an MK 16 Mod 0 SCAR-L 5.56mm x 45mm carbine /assault rifle with CQCs [ten inch barrel] for close quarters fighting and a 30 round magazine that featured a Mk 13 Mod 0 40mm grenade launcher, scope, and sound suppressor. They were dressed in black with balaclava hoods and soft soled shoes. They reached the doors of three apartments presumed to house number of violent offenders.

The lead sergeant major gave three clicks on his mic, and the units swept into the three apartments behind a cloud of flash bangs and smoke bombs. The soldiers were wearing breathing masks and goggles which protected them from the acrid smoke. The perps were unsuspecting and woke up in a dream induced and actual fog. Some tried to extract handguns from beneath their pillows; some tried to roll to the floor and into a fighting stance as they had been trained. Some were too slow to realize what was happening. Every one of them died in the first five seconds of the "fight". No law enforcement or military personnel were killed or wounded—the same as in the Washington DC mission.

It was too soon for elation, but the Situation Room officers were all smiles. They waited for the next reports from around the country. By 1900 hours, all units had checked in reporting successes. In sum, several hundred of the WOWs were killed, fifty-six were detained, some critically wounded. Nearly a ton of contraband—including a pickup truck bed amount of white powder—was confiscated. The intel coming from the survivors was probably the most valuable asset obtained. Not a single legal American was injured or killed.

President Daniels gave a silent "*thanks*".

The putative insurrection was far from over, but by the end of the day, the vicious hydra had no head.

Sybil took a deep breath and ordered, "Send in the cavalry. Tell them to be careful not to get hurt."

For the next three days, police, soldiers, fire fighters, prosecuting attorneys, and select embedded journalists, invaded the several worlds of criminal insurrectionists and exterminated most of them, captured over 2,000 of them, watched another thousand or so vanish into the debris and chaos, and hauled nearly 3,000 to hospitals and insta-care units wearing flex-cuffs. The latter were triaged as the least urgent or important.

In the aftermath, Sybil slept for two full days; the National Guard backed up police units to restore order to the now highly chastened neighborhoods; and fire inspectors, building inspectors, and construction experts, combed the ruins. It would take months before full reports would be forthcoming. All emergency and major disaster declarations are made solely at the discretion of the president of the United States. So—over the next year—FEMA sent accounting information to Sybil for her information—which she made public immediately. The numbers mounted rapidly—45° on the y-axis in a plane Cartesian coordinate system—for the first six months, then began to taper off. After the amount flattened out, the costs continued for seven years and impaired the US national economy for twenty years.

Sybil knew that this great misfortune for the United States would likely doom her presidency even though she was only days into her first term and—by any objective measure—she could not have had control over the initiating events.

Once the immediate danger subsided and the martial and police forces had regained the rule of law and social order, Sybil made a tour to six of the worst damaged areas with the governors of the respective states to assess at close range the extent of financial, infrastructural, architectural, and human costs. It was heart wrenching; and she gained a clear vision of what a great loss the country had suffered. It became all the more evident when hot spots began to occur around the world that the US could not help. At least for the time being, the United States would not be the "world's cop".

Brexit enthusiasts took advantage of America's plight to mount a street and parliament campaign against the US. Some went so far as to demand that Great Britain finish the job of attacking the US now at her weakest hour. Iran and North Korea made noises but did nothing provocative for the moment. Fortunately for him, his country, and, indeed, the rest of the civilized world, nothing was heard from former Prime Minister Benjamin Wood-Jackson

After her assessment tour, Sybil arranged to make another speech to the nation on television:

"My fellow Americans, friends from all over the world within the sound of my voice; my brothers and sisters. As you are well aware, the United States of America has been beset by a calamity from within. We thank all of you who have rendered assistance, and we will not forget. We are grateful to the Peoples Republic of China, to Germany, and to the European Union, for loaning us the funds to see our way through this difficult time. This is the equivalent of the Marshall Plan in reverse. Thank you.

"We have more difficulties ahead; the damage our country has suffered is not just to our treasured buildings, or to our innocent citizens personally, but to our economy. Our national debt is expected to rise another three trillion US dollars by the time the accounting is completed. Our businesses, churches, schools, highways, and our important infrastructure, have been damaged. However, our credit ratings remain as strong as ever; our ability to pay our debts on time and in full remains intact. More importantly, the will of the Americans is a powerful and unbroken as ever. This is not our darkest hour; we have seen worse; and we will overcome.

"There are those who have made threats against us during what they deem to be our weakened state. I tell you this as president; friend or enemy, we can defend ourselves at the same remarkable level we could before all of this happened. Do not make the mistake of underestimating our capability or our indominable will. We are Americans! God bless America!"

The year-end treasury report to the president gave sobering evidence for what the president had said. The unemployment rate had risen to twenty-five percent; the federal reserve interest rate had leveled out at zero over the six months following the attacks. The interest payments on the national debt–not even including any thought of paying down on the principle–had climbed to $110 billion per day. The treasury secretary tried weekly and weakly to reassure the worried president that it would by a far distant day before the US would default on its loans. Still… Sybil could not shake her foreboding.

Sybil was not panicked nor particularly concerned over the potential for her administration to last only long enough to finish out President Willets' final two years had he lived long enough to see its completion. She did feel like she should begin pinching pennies, at least figuratively speaking. Great Britain owed the United States and many of its citizens recompense for the damage they caused during the infamous attacks on our soil, our ships, and our people.

In her meeting with the British prime minister in the earliest days of her presidency, she had been lenient about the issues of reparation. She was no longer feeling so lenient. They owed us for the damage caused; and now, she was growing determined to see that they paid down serious money and very soon. The entire principle would have to wait until the weakened little island country could regain its financial feet enough to pay interest regularly and to begin to return the principle to the United States.

It was in that frame of mind that she put in a call to Prime Minister Lord Blancomb.

# CHAPTER SEVEN

The switchboard at No. 10 Downing alerted the prime minister that the president of the United States was calling and asked to speak only to him. PM David Lord Blancomb had been dreading this call and had been expecting it on the same day as the Country Cousins had their troubles but before it became global news. He had the operator hold President Daniels off for five or ten minutes while he collected himself and could get the Chancellor of the Exchequer to be able to listen in.

He sounded breathless when he said, "Hello, Madam President. Sorry to keep you. I was working out."

"Good for you, David. I have had to let myself go a bit of late. A little busy."

"I can only imagine, Sybil. I'm happy you could find time to give me a call."

"David, we are friends and will be as long as we can be candid and courteous. It is my intention to be so now. It cannot come as news to you that, the United States treasury has taken a severe beating in the last month or so. We are becoming indebted excessively to counties and institutions we would prefer not to do any more business with than absolutely necessary. I don't like the hold they are gaining."

"The Chinese?"

"Yes, mostly, but lately we are having to keep making overtures to the Saudis and even the Russians. They are quite cordial about it, but I see the day coming soon when both them and the Chinese will require that strings be attached before they give us more funding to keep our democracy afloat. My expectation is that the first thing we are going to see is a fairly large increase in the loan interest rate. If our credit ratings go down with Equifax, Dun and Bradstreet, Experian, Moody's, or the S&P, they will have all the leverage they need to hold us up like bandits. My popularity levels are falling every week, and it won't be long before there will be a groundswell movement to get me out of office. Can you see where this is going, David?"

"Unfortunately, I do. I want to help you personally, Sybil, and your country more than you can know."

"But?"

"Yes, 'but'…I am sure you are aware of the state of Her Majesty's Treasury. If you have doubts about my honesty, you can speak directly to the Second Lord of the Treasury who is listening in right now."

"I have no reason to doubt your veracity, David. But I do know where your fiduciary interests lie, and I don't expect you to have any preference for me or my country over your own. I don't need to remind you about the recent unfortunate losses inflicted on the United States by your predecessor. It is my opinion and that of everyone in Washington with a law license that you owe us a serious sum of money despite of the fact that no one–including me–has any reason to doubt that you were anything but a hero in your actions to prevent an all-out war."

"Again, there's a 'but'. But... I don't know where we can scrape up much of a down payment on the reparations now."

"Come now, Second Lord, can you tell me with a straight face that you do not have a rainy-day fund some-where in your treasury?"

The Chancellor replied quickly, "Madam President, I am sure you have good intelligence sources who have already told you what kind of money—and especially, liquidity—we have. If you took our entire treasury, you could pay off your debts, but our nation would fall. That is not in any of our best interests, Madam President. The PM and I should have gotten together sooner to make deci-sions that can help the survival of both our nations. But, we are here today, remiss in the fact that we have not done anything towards that kind of decision making. Please do not think us rude or procrastinating when we ask for five hours to get the data. We will call you back before bedtime tonight. You have my promise."

"And mine," the PM echoed.

"I trust you as I said in the beginning. I need to have a figure that will put a smile on my friends' faces and will not be so paltry as to give my enemies more fodder to come at me."

After the president and the prime minister disconnected, he kept the Lord Chancellor on the line.

"David, I already know the figures as well as you. Help me with information about cuts we can make to give the Cousins something they can use, but is not so much that our Britannia's economy is wrecked, all right?"

"I will, Prime Minister; you won't like it; but I will comply fully and honestly before all is said and done. How did we ever allow ourselves to get into this position, Prime Minister?

"I know the answer, of course; it was swinish avarice and cretinous stupidity. Too bad that bonehead Wood-Jackson didn't accidently fall out of a high-flying helicopter before he ever got to Ten Downing.

"You're right, Sir, but my crying over spilt milk does no good now. I'll get back to you before tea-time with what I think we can gouge out of the treasury and not sink ourselves. They'll just have to accept it. You have serious political and diplomatic credit with the new president. Maybe this is the time to spend it."

"Thanks, David, you're a brick."

"Welcome. If I didn't know you better, I would think you meant that as a compliment."

They both laughed and hung up.

Sybil next called in Dr. Devon Greyshire, who had reluctantly agreed to head up the National Rebuilding Coalition, as it was now called.

"What an honor, Madam President. How can I help?"

"Now, there's an attitude I can applaud, Devon. I want to apprise you of the money situation in the country that may impact your project. There is always something that competes for reconstruction, repair, or even maintenance, money for the infrastructure. We have just suffered a huge blow, which is not news to you. I also just got off the line with the Brits about reparations. I think they will come up with something, but not close to enough. I will get as much of that to you as I can. Hang on there, My Friend. Keep your volunteers' spirits up. We have to keep this project going as much and as fast as we can."

"Roger that, Madam President. They are good people, one and all. They will understand, but they won't under-stand forever. I am all but certain that there is rainy-day money around somewhere. Convince Congress and the treasury of that and why the infrastructure needs it."

"My next call is to Frank Caldwell over at Treasury. I hate doing it, because I always get down in the dumps after I hear him out."

"I don't envy you the job you inherited, Madam President, but I wish you God speed."

"Greetings, Mr. Secretary," Sybil said as soon as Frank Caldwell picked up the phone. "I have something import-ant to speak to you about, Frank."

"And not just 'how about them Capitals? I'm guessing," Secretary Caldwell joked.

"A trifle more serious and numerical. I have real trouble getting straight answers from the Hill. How much liquid money do we have in the treasury—'liquid' as in available over a three week period on my say so?"

"I'll have my people check. Should be able to get back to you in two hours' time. That fast enough?"

"Yes. Thanks, Frank; I'll owe you a marker."

"I don't forget that kind of thing. I'll think of some way to use your marker. Try and get some sleep, Chief; you must have a sleep debt as bad as the national one."

As promised, Treasury Secretary Frank Caldwell called the president on her secure line before close of the business day.

"Madam President, not only do I have an answer to the question you asked about the availability of large sums of money, but I also took the liberty of consulting legal and Constitutional scholars on the subject of your powers to obtain and use money without going through Congress.

"Ah, Frank, one of these days I'll come over to Treasury and kiss your Harvard Business School ring."

"I'll hold you to that. So, first the money: we have plenty of money, and you can have what you need. Second, the caution is about Congress and its thorny little Constitutional mandate to control the legislation of money matters and its dispersion for the most part. Read Article I, Section 8, which specifies the powers of Congress in great detail. The power to appropriate federal funds is known affectionately as the "power of the purse." In particular, the Constitution gives Congress great authority over the executive branch, which must appeal to Congress for all of its funding."

"And, that's the good news for me? I can hardly wait to hear the bad."

"Hold your horses, Madam President, there's more. There is a thing called impoundment. That is an act by a president whereby he or she can take advantage of the rule not to spend money that has been appropriated by Congress. By a series of actions and reactions between presidents and Congress, the president's ability to *indefinitely reject* congressionally *approved spending* was removed. Supplemental appropriations bills for disasters or national emergencies—for which there are *beau coup* examples—increase funding for activities that were *already funded in previous appropriations bills*, or they provide new funding for *unexpected expenses.*

Supplemental appropriations bills also provide funding for recovering from unexpected natural disasters like hurricanes or civil unrest. Are you following my drift, Madam President? This is the president's great power to get around Congress, and there are so many precedents that you will not even have to have a legal battle to get the money you need. Just say the magic words, 'disaster and/or emergency'.

"Recently–as if it were planned by you–the budget Fy 2020 provided funding to expand FinCEN›s role in fighting cybercrime, and the President's Budget Discretionary Appropriations Request constituted an order for Treasury to achieve its post-FIRRMA/CFIUS mission requirements. It just so happens that the majority of *already funded* programs have closed, and the need for a stand-alone audit has diminished to nearly nil.

"So, Madam President, you—as president—already have authority granted by Congress to get your needed funding. You can issue executive orders, which have the force of law but do not have to be further approved by Congress. Now–should they balk–there is this little presidential perk: in times of emergency—largely defined and ordered by the president—he or she (meaning you) can override Congress and issue executive orders with almost limitless power. Let me repeat that; 'limitless power'. The critics of the Constitution have bemoaned the fact since the republic was established, and subsequent re-readings and votes have amounted to a governance theory that reads: 'The president has not just some executive powers, but *the* executive power–the whole thing'."

"This is like my birthday, anniversary, and Christmas, all rolled into one. I applaud you, my learned guru. I have to ask—though–is it possible for the executive branch of the US government to spend money on something like a climate czar in the face of a law *specifically banning funds* from being used for that purpose as the Republicans have done? Another–more sinister example would be–could President Ronald Reagan have avoided the Iran-Contra scandal–at least the part involving sending money from the arms sales to the Contra–simply by issuing a "signing statement" claiming that the Boland Amendment–banning aid to the Contras–interfered with executive authority; and therefore–he was free to ignore it?"

"That gets into murky waters, but I am surprised that he didn't make a serious try. Anyhow, what you are after is nowhere near as thorny as the Iran-Contra issue. The voting public is definitely in favor of you solving the country's problems, and Congress almost never votes against a measure so popular. Remember, elected officials almost never vote for or against any measure which is split down ideological lines near 50:50. Not to be unduly jaded–but in my long career–I have seen politicians exercising their efforts to anything that gets them re-elected, and nothing that would harm their chances of continuing incumbency."

# CHAPTER EIGHT

President John F. Kennedy was once asked how it felt to be the most powerful person in the world. He took a moment to pause, then answered, "I have such power that I can order almost anything I want…and I can get almost nothing done, especially with any speed." Newly appointed President Sybil Norcroft Daniels was a quick study, and she was coming to a firm understanding of President Kennedy's piece of pragmatic wisdom.

The Chancellor of the Exchequer, Second Lord of the Treasury Malcolm David Leonard McTavish, returned President Daniel's call shortly after teatime in London—7:21 PM. It was 2:21 PM in Washington, DC.

"Thank you for taking the time to talk to me. I believe that I have some good news for you; not great news, but positive at least. I won't bore you and will avoid whining, but we can free up somewhere in the neighborhood of 34.4 and a half billion £ towards our debt by selling off some of our gold reserve and relinquishing some royal properties and nationally owned property. Her majesty has made a generous contribution, 'glad to be of help' she says."

"My quick calculation is that's about forty-five billion USD. That sound about right, David?"

"Yes, Ma'am. We can have it transferred to your treasury department inside of two weeks, 'God willin' and the creek don't rise' as they say down south in your country."

Sybil laughed. That is a great piece of news. Remember that you have a real friend in me and my country. I know this won't sit well with your voting public, especially the populist voters. I firmly hope we can both get through all of this."

"I'll scrounge up some more. There are some peerages that could end; some excess jobs held by aristocrats for prestige sake, and there's always Benjamin Lord Wood-Jackson's summer place, Lion's Lair, in the uplands that he might like to donate. We can always get the queen to throw in some of her excess furniture and pictures, I suppose."

"Lot's of luck with the latter," Sybil said, laughing with the second lord.


Sybil called for an emergency cabinet meeting and asked the CJCS, the Speaker of the House, the Majority Leader of the Senate, and the Principle Leader of the Bureau of the Budget, to attend with all the data they had on hand related to the debt burden the United States had recently acquired, and a generous estimate of what the cost of repairing the damage done by the rioters, their supporters, and the criminal conspiracy, behind it all.

"Thank you for coming on such notice. Let me begin with some fairly good news. I have been in contact with Prime Minister, Lord Blancomb and the Chancellor of the Exchequer of Great Britain today. With some time to check their bank accounts, they came up with an amount of forty-five billion dollars they can pay down on their reparations debt to us. They expect that amount to be transferred to our treasury department in less than two weeks."

There was hearty applause. A little good news went a long way during this awful period of time.

"Now, I want to turn the time over to Frank Caldwell, our resourceful secretary of the treasury and Lisa Brownell, the Principle Leader of the budget bureau. They have been in contact with many of you and some university professors and other economists to come up with data on what the recent insurrection has cost us and will cost as the future develops. I will have a few comments when he finishes, then, we will discuss how much we can take from the treasury, where and when it can be spent. By the close of business today, we will begin paying for restoration."

The Speaker of the House opened her mouth to speak, but President Daniels held up her hand in a gesture for her to hold her thought.

"So, give us the bad news, Lisa and Frank. I don't know if we can take it but give us the unvarnished version anyway."

The secretary and the principle leader tag-teamed to present a synopsis of the data from their several sources via a slide presentation from the treasury's laptop. Mr.

Caldwell passed out comb binders with the extensive data and a consensus synopsis prepared by the secretary and the principle leader personally. The gist of the immensely detailed report was that the overall cost of the treasonous destruction inflicted on the United States by its own citizens was a little north of $2 Trillion, give or take a few billion. The cost of the British predations amounted to $700 Billion.

Even the members of Congress who were used to wasting billions on pet projects were shocked into silence.

President Daniels gave her audience a few minutes to digest the huge mouthful they had just swallowed, then she made her few, but determinative comments.

"Now, ladies and gentlemen, we come to the moment of truth. How are we going to pay for all of this? In practical fact, we have two disasters slash emergencies. We can start with the $45 billion from the Brits; but, for all intents and purposes, that money has already been spent; that is, it is absolutely ear-marked to repair the damage they inflicted. And…it will not pay for direct and indirect human damages.

"Several dozen lawsuits are already in the pipeline. We could further increase our already stratospheric national debt by taking out more international loans. Our credit is still good, but I can't say how long that will last. We could raise taxes, maybe ten or even fifteen percent across the board, and that would cover the entirety. However, that has to happen soon. Our bills and our need for repairs are now and cannot be put off for weeks or months as is likely to happen as any iteration of a bill makes its weary way through the mires of Congress."

The Speaker opened her mouth again but thought better of it.

"Similarly, we cannot obtain what we need by a national belt tightening. That would be too little, and too late.

"Are we going to become a bankrupt little has-been nation as a result of all of this, Madam President? Good grief what will we tell the American people?" Douglas Williams, the Secretary of Labor spoke up in a strained voice.

The Speaker of the House and the Majority Leader of the Senate spoke at the same time using almost identical language, "You can forget about tax increases, Madam President. This is a mid-term election year. A tax increase bill has less chance of passing that does the proverbial snowflake in hell."

"Hold onto that thought," Sybil said.

The Secretary of Commerce, Rudolf Berkowitz Auerbach, spoke next, "Madam President, the sheer size of the national debt that would occur if we borrowed that much more indebtedness would have two results: first, our credit rating would drop, no matter how hard we try to convince the world's financiers that we are still altogether solvent. The immediate result of that would be that our great friends—the People's Republic of China—would become the largest and most successful economy in the world. We would likely fall to third, below Germany. That is unthinkable.

"To say the least, the American people are restive. Any of your so-called solutions might just tip-over the most angry of the already distrustful citizens to head towards secession, maybe anarchy, or to desire to link up with bigger stronger economies like the Russians, the Germans, the Chinese, or maybe even the European Union. Our recent experience might lead us to the conclusion that a secession movement could create a real bullet-firing civil war, not unlike what President Lincoln faced. How, on earth, did we ever get to this point?"

Senate Majority Leader Nichols put it as bluntly as he could to President Daniels, "Madam President, meaning no disrespect and not making any suggestions; but, as I see it, you will be impeached by a bipartisan majority if you can't pull a rabbit out of the hat."

"Thank you all for your comments. It so happens that I do have a figurative rabbit in my hat—a viable solution."

That perked up the interest of every red-faced, anxious, sweating, person in the room.

"Well, let's hear it," Speaker Zimbrowski said dubiously and with arched eyebrows.

"I have given this more thought and sleepless nights than any decision I have made in my whole life, my friends. What I propose is that I solve the conundrum by a fiat…a presidential order."

"What?" screeched the Speaker. "You may be new to the presidency or even to America, but I am here to instruct you. We are ruled by a set of laws called the Constitution. Let me summarize. Only the Congress—not the president—can legislate or appropriate money. Your apparent ignorance on the issue can be forgiven since you are barely into the first one-hundred days of your administration, but ignorance is no excuse. If you ask for money, we, in the Congress, will give your request due consideration; and, Madam President, that will take time, probably months. Furthermore, there is no way that you will get anywhere near the figures you have quoted."

"Have you finished, Madam Speaker?" the president asked using her famous icy-calm voice.

"For now," Zimbrowski replied.

"Then, I am here to tell you not only that I can, but I will give a legal presidential order; and it will be obeyed with all the force of federal law. To remove any ignorance many of you may have on the subject, I am going to have Secretary Caldwell and Leader Brownell instruct you—to deliver the *coup de grâce* as it were."

The two well-informed financial officers proceeded to tell the assemblage what they had told President Daniels earlier in the day.

Again, they tag-teamed; this time it was brief Cliff's Notes versions of Constitutional law viz a viz the relationship of the legislative and the executive branches as it applies to finance.

"First, as a matter of accounting this morning, we have plenty of money; and the president can have what she needs.

"Second, there is indeed a Constitutional mandate to control the legislation of money matters and its dispersion for the very most part. Article I, Section 8, which specifies the powers of Congress in great detail. The power to appropriate federal funds is commonly known as the "power of the purse." The Constitution gives Congress great authority over the executive branch, which must appeal to Congress for all of its funding."

"I just told you that; it's nothing new," interrupted Speaker Zimbrowski, preparing to mount her high horse.

"Bear with me a bit longer, Madam Speaker, there's more. I need to acquaint you with the principle of impoundment—it's Constitutional. That is an act by a president whereby he or she can take advantage of the rule not to spend money that has been appropriated by Congress. By a series of actions and reactions between presidents and Congress, the president's ability to reject *indefinitely* congressionally *approved spending* was removed. Supplemental appropriations bills for disasters or national emergencies—for which there are *beau coup* examples–increase funding for activities that were *already funded in previous appropriations bills*, or they provide new funding for *unexpected expenses*. Now, everyone, we are getting to the nitty-gritty."

"This had better be good," the Majority Leader said with emphasis which the Speaker punctuated with her famous raised eyebrow and facial grimace expression.

"I'll hold you to that. So, first the money: we have plenty of money, and you can have what you need. Second, the caution is about Congress and its thorny little Constitutional mandate to control the legislation of money matters and its dispersion for the most part. Read

Article I, Section 8, which specifies the powers of Congress in great detail. The power to appropriate federal funds is known affectionately as the "power of the purse." In particular, the Constitution gives Congress great authority over the executive branch, which must appeal to Congress for all of its funding."

"And, that's the good news for me? I can hardly wait to hear the bad."

"Hold your horses, Madam President, there's more. There is a thing called impoundment. That is an act by a president whereby he or she can take advantage of the rule not to spend money that has been appropriated by Congress. By a series of actions and reactions between presidents and Congress, the president's ability to *indefinitely reject* congressionally *approved spending* was removed. Supplemental appropriations bills for disasters or national emergencies—for which there are *beau coup* examples—increase funding for activities that were *already funded in previous appropriations bills*, or they provide new funding for *unexpected expenses*. Supplemental appropriations bills also provide funding for recovering from unexpected natural disasters like hurricanes or civil unrest. Are you following my drift, Ladies and Gentlemen? This is the president's great power to get around Congress, and there are so many precedents that you will not even have to have a legal battle. President Daniels will get the money she needs. Practically speaking, all she has to do is to say the magic words, 'disaster and/or emergency'.

"As if that might not be enough, recently the budget Fy 2020 provided funding to expand FinCEN›s role in fighting cybercrime, and the President›s Budget Discretionary Appropriations Request constituted an order for Treasury to achieve its post-FIRRMA/CFIUS mission requirements. It just so happens that the majority of *already funded* programs have closed, and the need for a stand-alone audit has diminished to nearly nil.

"So, the president, you—in this case, Sybil Norcroft Daniels, already has the necessary authority *granted by Congress* to get your needed funding. She can issue executive orders forthwith, which have the force of law but do not have to be further approved by Congress. Now, should Congress balk, there is an important presidential perk: in times of emergency—largely defined and ordered by the president—he or she—President Daniels–*can override Congress* and issue executive orders with almost limitless power. Let me repeat that; 'limitless power'. The critics of the Constitution have bemoaned the fact since the republic was established, and subsequent re-readings and votes have amounted to a governance theory that reads: 'The president has not just some executive powers, but *the* executive power–the whole thing'.

"I repeat, supplemental appropriations bills also provide funding for recovering from unexpected natural disasters like hurricanes or civil unrest. This is the president's great power to get around Congress, and there are so many precedents that her power is unassailable. Remember, the key words, 'disaster and/or emergency' and the statement that ultimately governs the United States government–'The president has not just some executive powers, but *the* executive power–the whole thing'."

"It will never hold up. We will fight you to the end," the members of Congress and the Senate asserted vociferously.

President Daniels and her cabinet members smiled beatifically.

# CHAPTER NINE

As she knew she would, Sybil had poked a finger into the congressional hornets' nest. Both houses and both parties saw their sacrosanct privileges being trampled upon. She got her $Two trillion with no difficulty from the treasury but brought down on herself a firestorm of attacks in the media, in the halls of Congress, and among the far right and left wing printing presses. The *Enquirer* ran a headline *"Pres. Caught in Love Triangle"*, and another, accompanied by a photograph of *"New President Norcroft-Daniels Naked at the Beach with Gangland Boss."* Following the advice of her personal and the White House attorneys, she filed a lawsuit for defamation of character and libel. Her ask was for $1 Billion.

Whatever else was accomplished by the media attention, Sybil Norcroft Daniels dominated the airways and print paths almost without precedent. Her name and photographs—including those not photoshopped—were in the news literally hundreds of times a day. Despite the fact that she never granted an interview and never appeared in public functions for the two weeks following the treasury handing over the $2 Trillion, she became the P.T. Barnum, Donald Trump, Britney Spears, Paris Hilton, Michael Jackson, and Ben Affleck's Engagement to Jennifer Lopez, all rolled into one, for the media; and none of it sought after or appreciated.

The saving grace for the determined new president was the efficiency, skill, and honesty, with which her appointees carried out the confusing, confrontational, and thankless, task of creating plans and contracts, overcoming legal, union, and activist group, impediments, and finally getting demolition and reconstruction underway, all the while keeping a monk-like C.P.A. eye on every penny going out. They worked long hours for little or no pay, and absolutely no notoriety.

Like the WWII engineers who flocked to Washington DC to contribute their time and talents when the country was going into crisis mode and the «Pioneer troops», a hand-selected unit of volunteer Army combat engineers trained in jungle warfare, knife fighting, and unarmed jujitsu techniques. They worked in camouflage, and cleared jungle, prepared routes of advance and established bridgeheads for the infantry, as well as demolishing enemy installations. President Daniels determined to instill the same dedication to volunteerism in the people who flocked to the capital to help reconstruct wounded America.

Once the planning and other logistical necessities were ironed out and well in place, President Daniels again addressed the nation on all the television networks. She outlined the extent and location of damages, the need for demolition and rebuilding, the cost of the federal and state enterprise, and the selfless volunteerism that was going to make the effort a success. She made an oblique reference to the reparations contribution by Great Britain and explained the planned payment rules to the military, to the base cities which sustained injury, and the plans to compensate the families of people killed and injured by the British misadventure.

Charles Daniels—the husband of the president, as he preferred to be called—was, as always throughout the adventure of their marriage–her steadying rock. She had to appear to be a pillar of strength and leadership to the public, to the military as commander-in-chief, and to the elected and appointed officials of the government—many of whom did not wish her well, quite the contrary.

Sybil made the end-of-day weary trek to the residence where Charles, Cerisse, Drake Farrer, and, Sybil Aminita, and Bonheur were waiting in an irregular and wriggling reception line to welcome her home.

"Gramma, gramma," the two children shouted unable to contain themselves any longer.

Sybil Aminita was just learning to put two and three word sentences together.

She said, "Gamma, my needs a hug!"

She got two.

Bonheur, whose vocabulary indicated a precocity–perhaps from being around adults too much–asked, "Gramma, do I have to call you 'Missus President' like all the men in suits?"

"It's 'Madam President, Bonheur," reminded Charles.

"Oh, right. But, can't you just be my Gramma?"

"Of course, I can. I will always be your Gramma. I will only be 'Madam President' for a while. And, I think you need a hug and to have your neatly combed hair mussed up."

He giggled and tried to escape having his hair mussed, but in a couple of minutes the whole family was having a good bedtime wrestle on the floor. The release from the physical activity and unbridled love was refreshing, and Sybil felt less worn-out than she had all day.

Drake and Cerisse gave Gramma hugs and warm cheek good night kisses, and the children excitedly awaited their turns. Then the parents dragged the reluctant children off to bed. Charles kissed Sybil seriously, and helped her into her pajamas. It was eleven o'clock, and she could barely keep her eyes open long enough to brush her teeth. She could no longer control her emotions and had a good cathartic cry in Charles's arms before collapsing into a dreamless sleep.

The next morning's PDB centered on China, Russia, England, and the status of the nation's preparations for reconstruction. Her successor DCIA, Martin Obershauer, DNI Admiral David P. Jacobsen, and Lt. Gen. Paul R. Reynolds, Director of the National Security Agency, tag teamed the presentation which lasted a very full fifteen minutes.

Director Obershauer told the assembled national security team that, "Our friends in Beijing have two trains of communication going. In Mandarin, they are telling their people that the haughty and once mighty Americans have come to the Great Leaders of the Party hat-in-hand to have their country—which is now the most powerful economy in the world as a result of the party's years of struggle—and the party and the government will capitalize on that objective fact with tenacity and patience. This is "the Chinese century" has become the red banner mantra all around the country. The PLA [People's Liberation Army] has been staging fairly bellicose military parades for the past two weeks in Beijing, Shanghai, and Guangzhou, with a visual message that is intended for the civilian masses. Of course, their communications with us in English paint a far more docile and friendly character."

The DNI added that all of the US intelligence services are picking up increased secure traffic from Russia, the Middle-East, China, Iran, and North Korea.

"The general consensus is that America is more vulnerable than ever before, at least economically. Russia and China are both making overtures to the Islamic radical organizations to establish stronger relationships to weaken the 'Great Satan' even further. Our most serious alarm is that there is considerable traffic between Riyadh and Moscow with talk about a united effort to convince the OPEC nations to mount a shut-off of the flow of oil to the western nations to create a world-wide depression comparable to their accomplishment in 1973. The purpose is to injure the American economy even further and worse than the Europeans, Asians, and Middle-Easterners will suffer.

The Saudis seem to be reticent to have their involvement known by the public, but the Russians want to be seen as the saviors for the rest of the world, other than the US and for that to be very public when the time is appropriate."

Lt. Gen. Reynolds the DIRNSA [Director of the National Security Agency], reported on the status of the unrest and its aftermath throughout the country.

"We are continuing to mount a police action with military officers and enlisted having been tasked with arrest authority as well as their military duties. I am pleased to report that the cooperation of federal, state, and local, law enforcement is very nearly seamless. Military and police have been able to agree on principles of law enforcement despite the differences between the two ways of approaching problems. Not only is the amount of insurrection unrest now quiet with only rare acts of terrorism, but the crime rate throughout the nation has dropped precipitously and continues to decrease every week. The worst offenders against the nation are for the most part gone. The rest are thoroughly cowed.

"There is a growing recognition in even the previously most crime ridden areas of the value of cohesive and functioning families. We are even beginning to see the dawning of cooperation with police officers on the part of people who have been raised in families and neighborhoods where the police were seen as brutal, unfair, and the enemy. We have a formal study underway to determine the best way to continue this salutary state of affairs."

The president had the last word as always.

"Thanks gentlemen. You have done your work under most trying circumstances, and I trust you to continue despite any amount of criticism you get from an unappreciative public. Know that I always have your back—to use an overworked phrase, but one that I mean sincerely. Your information is disturbing. I plan to have my advisors work with me to prepare a speech to the nation which outlines where we go from here in this tumultuous and threatening times. Each of you will likely be contacted several times.

"Now to some specifics. As to the Chinese, Director Obershauer, Director Jacobsen, we need you, the FBI, DARPA, and the NSA, to gather information with an intensity akin to the preparation of an unyielding prosecutor. I will confront the PRC leadership shortly, and I want to have the evidence in front of me to bring them up short.

"Gen. Reynolds, I want you to get with State, and to arrange meetings with the Russians. Have evidence in hand to show them that we are well-aware of their clandestine communications which are averse to us. Assure the Russians that the sanctions will remain in place until and unless they relinquish their presence in the Crimea an in Eastern Ukraine. I will hold meetings with the dictator, Putin, to reinforce our demands; but I want the ammunition from you to help me to be effective. Also, get the Department of Defense on board to use their influence to convey the fact that the US is not a paper tiger. I will give Homeland Defense a call to get them to engage more actively with the NSA to bring any and all remaining miscreants to heel.

"Seal the borders like never before; we cannot afford to have criminals creep in to stir the insurrection pot any longer."

"Madam President, do we have the money to do all this?" Director Jacobsen asked.

"Thanks for asking that pertinent question, Paul. The answer is 'yes'. This is a formally declared national emergency; so, I can exercise my presidential powers to obtain whatever we need from the treasury without getting permission from the legislature. We have more than adequate funds available, and I have no intention of being stingy."

Director Obershauer asked, "It's not exactly the CIA's business, but are you sure your presidential orders can survive the attacks that are sure to be launched by the legislature to force you to back down.

"And thanks to you, Frank. Again, the answer is yes. The secretary of the treasury and I have done our due diligence and have written opinions by his department, the White House lawyers, and Constitutional scholars, that I have all the power I need under Article I, Section 8. Maybe, in the end, SCOTUS will have the final word; but the Constitution is clear. I intend to use it as my shield in the inevitable battle. I will not let petty partisan politics or nit-picking of the Constitution by my opponents to rule the day. Count on me."

# CHAPTER TEN

Sybil had prepared assiduously for this day of important confrontations. She was a quick and thorough learner from her days in medical school and while preparing to defend her doctoral dissertation. She was well aware that she was going to debate some of the most intelligent lawyers—people—in the country and several nations. She expected them to obfuscate and protest her evidence, to cast aspersions on her gender, her lack of governmental experience, and her age. At the age of forty-two when she took the presidential oath of office, she became the youngest person ever to become president. President John F. Kennedy—the previous holder of that distinction–was forty-three.

The first meeting of the day after the PDB—which only increased the general level of angst—was with the senior members of both houses, and both parties. Unlike their lackluster attention to punctuality in their congressional meetings, every one of the leaders invited arrived on time, attended by a staff lawyer, and carrying a heavy leather brief case.

"Welcome to the White House, my esteemed colleagues. We have considerable work to get through and will have to be succinct in our presentations. Knowing the issues that dominate today's agenda, I have invited Justice Leopold Draganoval of the Supreme Court to discuss the Constitution as it pertains to financial procurement from the treasury. I would like to refresh your memories about Justice Draganoval's résumé as it relates to the questions we shall argue today. Once he finishes, there will be a question and answer period of thirty minutes followed by presentations by anyone in attendance that desires to do so. Because of the numbers here, and in the interests of time, each speaker will be limited to fifteen minutes."

Not a single person other than the president had any intention of being limited by her time constraints; no one would ever be so prosaic as to interfere with a congressman or senator in the midst of delivering a timeless pronouncement.

President Daniels was prescient; she accurately read the thoughts in common of the self-important narcissists.

"Because one or two of us might forget the time restraints, I have asked the chief usher of the Senate to hold us to our limits."

She heard a few *sub rosa* groans.

With a winning smile, she said, "You're welcome."

Several could not help themselves and rewarded her with a little laugh.

Justice Draganoval presented a brief, lawyerly, and cogent, dissertation of the separation of the three branches of American government, the privileges and limitations, of each, and then a professorial explanation of the history and present-day employment of a president of government funding. He could have taken a page from Treasury Secretary Frank Caldwell's previous communication to Congress and the White House staff regarding presidential privileges hidden in Article I, Section 8. The members of Congress showed their intense disfavor by their united sulking faces.

Speaker of the House Zimbrowski had pushed her way to the front of the line of speakers and took her turn as if it were some sort of unwritten protocol. She presented a memorized script as if she had not been in the room when Justice Draganoval made his remarks. She made no allusion to Treasury Secretary Frank Caldwell's explanation given with her in a state of rapt attention.

Her concluding statement was also quite obviously scripted, "Madam President, I will stand at the doors of the treasury to prevent you from obtaining a dime for your pet project. I will defend the Constitution to my dying breath. You shall not prevail. If you push for this, or God forbid, succeed, I will see you impeached before you can carry out your attack on our republic."

President looked the speaker directly in the eyes and said with maddeningly calm poise… "Thank you, Madam Speaker."

The chief usher announced, "The honorable Senate Majority Leader Ralph Henry Nichols."

His speech was less of a harangue than the speaker's, but the message came from the same set of writers. In brief, he would never allow any president, let alone one who was never elected and a newcomer to violate the Constitutional separation of powers. He repeated his statement made when the president first made her announcement almost word for word.

"Madam President, you are making a terrible rookie mistake. I told you earlier: you will be impeached by a bipartisan majority if you proceed forward with this drastic scheme. The treasury is depleted by the recent attempted insurrection, and it will be years before we can recuperate. You can't squeeze blood out of turnip. You are still young in your presidency, Madam, and you can still repent and step back from the precipice."

Sybil politely thanked Leader Nichols and gave him a pleasant smile.

In the several hours that followed, the military officers heartily approved of their commander-in-chief's plan. Every lawyer in the room became a Constitutional scholar that day. The White House scholars sided with Sybil unreservedly, oddly enough. Their opinions were counterbalanced by the congressional attorney/newly made Constitutional scholars who expressed the same outrage at the president as their congressional employers had. It was a Mexican standoff. It remained to be seen which side would have to blink first.

Sybil's second meeting of the day was with the Russian, Saudi, and PRC, ambassadors, none of whom was any too happy to be summoned to the Oval Office. Not even the promise of White House sous chef, Suzie Granthem's, internationally famous pastry platter was enough to cut their feeling that they were headed to the principal's office for a spanking.

Sybil and new Secretary of State David de Leon stood to greet the ambassadors.

De Leon was an excellent choice to accompany the president. She had done so many times with former President Willets, and the ambassadors had no misapprehensions that this was going to be a cake walk for them. De Leon was every bit the world leader in appearance. He was tall, patrician, perfectly coiffed, and his clothes were New York City Bespoke bench-made perfect—dark, the finest fine woven wool, the brightest white Egyptian cotton shirt and Paul Malone black silk and gold striped tie and matching pocket square. His nails were freshly manicured and his handmade black calf leather shoes were new. They gave off a flash of light when caught in a lamp light. His face wore an indelible inscrutable expression—the perfect gambler's face with never a tell.

It was not the first time either the president or the secretary had met the ambassadors. No one in the room had any illusion that they were playing the game of diplomacy with anyone but the A team.

"Thank you coming to the White House on such short notice. We fully recognize that you are busy men, and we are similarly busy. I will get right down to brass tacks."

The Russian showed in his face that he had not understood the American colloquialism.

"Details," de Leon said softly.

"Yes, no small talk or chit-chat," the president added. "I don't suppose that I need to tell you that the United States has a truly extraordinary intelligence service. Bear that in mind when I tell you this. We are aware—in detail—that you and the Chinese have increased their encrypted chatter by a factor of four in the last two weeks. Our linguistic section has both fluent Russian speakers and Mandarin speakers. In fact, you could almost say that they are more than fluent; they speak each language as if they were native speakers.

"So, to make my story short, let me tell you what we have learned. You plan to destroy a section of the Iran-Turkish pipeline and blame in on the Islamic State. That loss will further injure the American economy until well after the damage has been repaired. The price of Iranian oil will go up, and they will prosper—at America's expense.

"Do I have your attention, yet, Gentlemen?"

The pale-faced ambassadors all nodded.

The president continued, "Now, what will America do about it is the real question when you get down to brass tacks. I will tell you. Tomorrow, Iran will cease all oil shipping to the north and west because they would rather see an easing of sanctions on them and a chance to sell oil to Europeans and the US at a substantially higher rate. The Chinese will obtain more of their oil from Middle-Eastern countries because several of the oil-producing are going to see a dangling carrot on a stick. The carrot is a promise that most favored nation status will be granted them on a probationary status. They will see a decrease in their unemployment rate by…I would guess 15-20 percent. Their dependence on Russian and Saudi oil will take a nose-dive. It's just business, right?

"For the Saudis—who have in mind to bring about an OPEC embargo against the United States—because they believe the Great Satan–as many of them call us–has found out their secret, and has taken steps to thwart their plans. They have struck a deal with the devil, you might say; and he will not let them off the hook easily. They are in for another period of belt tightening and rations."

"What are our options, Madam President?" the Russian Ivan Tarasoavich Dinlinal, asked trying not to betray his mounting concern.

"Cease and desist in these anti-American secret machinations or feel the wrath of a wounded by still capable and angry people. We are willing to forgive and to resume normal and mutual relationships. But…know that we are at the end of our patience. Our next response will not be any subtle expression of displeasure. It will be a memorable part of your history. Take that back to Putin and his oligarch co-conspirators."

Sheik Umar bin Wahhadi, the ambassador from Saudi Arabia, said with his usual syrupy ingratiating tone, "Madam President, surely you cannot believe that the Kingdom, your greatest and most faithful ally would seek to do harm to the United States in public or in secret…"

President Daniels halted his pablum-laced contribution mid-sentence.

"Sheik, we have full evidence of your perfidy, your conniving with OPEC to strike us when we are down. The kingdom miscalculated. We have tolerated your intolerance, your secret attacks on us and others not of your particular faith, and your flirtations with our avowed enemies long enough. This has never been said in public before, but we, alone, stand between your country and its vicious enemies to the very far right. We can erase that protection with the stroke of a pen. Do not push us again. Report this to Salman bin Abdulaziz Al Saud, King and Prime Minister of Saudi Arabia. Don't tone it down. I speak for the United States of America. Take care, minister.

President Daniels finished her workday with an in-camera meeting with her cabinet and the ten most senior members of the Senate and the House. For people not used to short and to-the-point meetings or to receiving a lecture, her off-the-cuff remarks were nearly unprecedented and—for most—quite unwelcome.

"My fellow Americans, this has been a most trying week or two. We have not faced such a crises for the American public, the economy, and the very persistence of our democracy since the Civil War or World War II. I, as president, whether you accept me or not having not been elected, I intend to use every power vouchsafed me to protect the Constitution, the American people, and its economy with every ounce of my energy and strength. I have sworn an oath to do so, and I take that oath entirely as a sacred obligation. Our economy is in ruins; I will acquire the necessary funding to see it restored. Our people are divided as never before; I will dispatch a veritable army of volunteers to help us reunite, whatever the monetary price or political cost for me. We are beset by foreign enemies who hope to capitalize on our misfortune to usurp our position as the guardian and protector of democracy and the worth of individuals around the world. So help me God, I will fight with all I have, and all we have to ensure that the phoenix that rises from the ashes of America today will be the powerful big brother again tomorrow.

"Go ahead with your deliberations, your vitriol if you must; but know that you have not inherited a weakling or a coward as your president. It is my opinion that you and the country will prosper as we work together as friends, but you will be shamed by your history if you defy me in this ultimately crucial moment."

Her listeners were stunned into silence. A majority of them vowed to launch a war against the upstart girl president.

# CHAPTER ELEVEN

Sybil's adrenaline rush did not dissipate before she returned to the residence that evening. Again, the family was waiting for her. Although they were not privy to the details of her skirmishes, they intuitively realized that their wife, mother, and grandmother had weathered a battering storm that day.

Charles said, "Sybil, you need a little TLC. Have you even eaten today? Were you able to have a moment to yourself? Did anyone support you?"

"My dear little husband, I could certainly use some unreserved TLC. And—now that you mention it–I am actually hungry."

"Good, Gramma, let's have some mac and cheese. I'm starving," cried four-year-old Sybil Aminita which broke the ice and caused Sybil's debilitating adrenaline hyper-state to evaporate.

Everyone had an affectionate laugh.

"Honey, that sounds great to me. How about some wieners to go along with that?"

Sybil Aminita looked serious, "Gramma, we are not supposed to say that. We should say 'hot dogs'."

The adults tried their best to maintain straight faces, but the innocence of her demand was so touching and funny, that it required another catharsis of laughter. The children had no idea what the laughing was about, but they laughed until they cried anyway.

The residence staff was a bit incredulous when they received the supper request, but they made the best mac, cheese, and hot dog supper the family had ever had.

Everyone was full but little two-year-old Bonheur wanted something more, "My wants some bascetti and some banilla."

He was sure the family was laughing at him and started to tear up. His gramma picked him up and danced with him; so, he got over any perceived slight quickly.

The next day began with all parties to the fight loaded for bear. The issue went to the House floor for debate and a vote by 0900. The debate brought out intense feelings and concerns on both sides of the aisle and—as unusual as it could be—political partisanship was not based on party, but on genuine concerns of the issues at hand: financing the reconstruction as quickly as possible versus the Constitutional issue over who controls the purse strings. By 1015, the House passed a bill to allow the president to procure emergency money from the treasury. The bill moved to the Senate at 1220, and heated debate raged over lunch and until it came to a vote at 1430.

President Daniels and her staff figuratively held their collective breaths until 1545 when the vote tally came in 51 to 49 against granting President Daniels access to the requested funding. The stalemate held through the night. By 0700 the next day, the House caved enough to make the first tally of the day, one vote in favor of refusal. Before noon, the Senate held fast at 51 to 49 against, and the bill went to the Oval Office.

Two minutes after the bill reached the president's desk, President Daniels made the first formal decision of her presidency. She vetoed the bill with a signature as large as John Hancock's on the *Declaration of Independence*.

The bill returned to both the House and the Senate; and with no debate, both houses came back with the same vote. President Daniels, Speaker Zimbrowski, and Majority Leader Nichols, unanimously sent a request to the Supreme Court for an expedited decision. The anticipated receipt of the request came to Justice Leopold Draganoval's desk. He recused himself because he had made a previous judgment on the case. The measure then landed on Chief Justice Chester Whitfield's desk. It was within his purview to adjudicate the case himself, but he decided to punt.

All nine members gathered in his office at 1655 and began to debate informally. It was brief, because Justice Draganoval's well prepared argument was inescapable. Every justice had a full evening schedule and wives who were tired of being understanding; so, at 1748, they voted 6 to 3 in favor of the president and the withdrawal of "any necessary funds to accomplish reconstruction of the United States".

It was too late that night to get the treasury secretary to release the funds, but Sybil called Secretary Caldwell at home and secured a promise to meet her at the treasury building in the morning. By 0900, President Daniels stood on the steps of the Main Treasury Building on 1500 Pennsylvania Avenue NW with a document granting her access to a sum of "Two $Trillion dollars, or as much as the president deems necessary to accomplish the goal of rebuilding the nation after the recent attempted insurrection."

The offices of the Congresspersons and Senators who had voted against her were well sound-insulated or else she could have heard their howls where she was standing.

# CHAPTER TWELVE

Every news outlet in the nation, large or small, newsprint or electronic transmission, television, radio, and the internet, carried two "breaking news" headlines: "SCOTUS Sides with Pres.—2 Trillion for Reconstruction" and "Speaker and Majority Leader Declare War on the Pres." President Daniels was neither surprised nor disappointed. She and her advisors had expected both responses and determined to go on with business as usual. Sybil took some small solace in the fact that there was not a third headline that read something like, "House Begins Debate on Impeachment."

The president had her secretary limit all appointments to those related to reconstruction and a small assortment of critical issues as approved by her. Sybil was a "good" president, i.e., she was good at delegation. She was determined that she would not micromanage and get into the trouble that President Carter had found himself by trying to go everywhere and do everything on his agenda. Nor would she ignore the issues like President Adams, who was absent from the White House for three months at a time.

The first morning of the new major American enterprise was spent in making sure that she requested appointments for the men and women she wanted to be in charge of the several issues involved and that those appointments would be quickly passed through the Senate for its "Advice and Consent".

The president could look down at her desk and see a document approving two trillion dollars plus for her pet project and at a printout of the Supreme Court's favorable decision. At mid-morning she came face-to-face with John Kennedy's conundrum: "I have such power that I can order almost anything I want...and I can get almost nothing done, especially with any speed." Every nomination she submitted became immediately bogged down in the Senate Committee on the Judiciary. Less than an hour passed after her several names were submitted for nomination before she received a courtesy transmission for the committee chair that the nomination had been received and would be given careful evaluation by the committee for advice and consent as required by the Constitution. However, the polite letters said, "in due time as necessary to evaluate such crucial nominations."

She recognized Majority Leader Nichols' hand in the foot-dragging posture and that this was his first salvo. She gathered her squadron of attorneys to determine her response.

White House Attorney, Cameron H. Matthews' first suggestion was, "Madam President, it would appear that the Leader and the committee chair intend to drag out the advice and consent process indefinitely to impede any progress you could make to get reconstruction underway. You could reply with legal demands, briefs, and rebuttals; but, all of that is expected and will use up a great deal of time.

"Or, you can invoke Senate Resolution 116 passed by the Senate on June 29, 2014 which allowed for an expedited process related to approval of a large number of specific presidential nominations—such as assistant secretaries, members of some boards and commissions, etc.—and thereby bypass the Senate subcommittees' approval process."

"They won't like it and will probably balk."

"Certainly true, but your attorneys agree that your next step is to do just that anyway. You can send nominations under the resolution to the chairpersons of the committees involved on presidential letter-head stationary under the heading, PRIVILEGED NOMINATIONS-INFORMATION REQUESTED. The staffs of those subcommittees need only verify that appropriate biographical and financial questionnaires have been submitted to and received back from the nominee in order to have the nominations considered by the full Senate."

"Still seems like a long process and another way to thwart my programs," President Daniels said.

"Democracy is messy, and much of it is a waste of time, often quite intentional. However, the overriding concept of the separation and checks and balances of the three branches of government has had that intention in mind since the Constitution was being drafted."

"Then, what? What if they get to the floor of the Senate, and the members continue of balk and to thwart me?"

"I suggest that we not get ahead of ourselves. We do have other remedies, but everyone of them has its drawbacks. Let us hope the senators choose to do the right thing."

Sybil followed her lawyers' recommendations and then had to wait with a little patience until the rusty wheels of Senate procedure began to creak along.

Dealing with the legislators was not the only problem facing Sybil. The NSA continued to monitor activity and amounts of oil flow in Middle-East pipelines. Five days after her stern talk with the Saudis and the Russians and later the Turks and sent a message via the Swiss to Iran, nothing had happened. Saudi oil exports remained at usual levels. The Russians had become silent in Crimea and Ukraine, which was a positive change from the bellicosity usually transmitted from the Russian Federation to its opponents in the two areas.

Instead of taking the path of most caution, President Daniels elected to communicate with the Saudis and the Russians before a reasonable period had passed to allow her to be convinced that the leaders of the two countries had truly acquiesced with her previous communication.

"Hello, Mr. President," Sybil said as soon as the Russian president's famous face appeared on her laptop screen.

"I hope you are well and that you and your family have escaped the latest flu season scares."

"We have thus far, Madam President. You know that many of my countrymen believe the flu scare is another hoax perpetrated by the hegemonist nations against us communists. This time, the intent seems to be to increase tensions between us and the People's Republic."

"However that might be, I am calling about the issue of the Saudi and Russian provocations and threats against America…"

"I have to protest…" Putin started to say.

"Not necessary, Mr. President. My call has a simple and positive intent. Those in my country tasked with monitoring oil flow report to me that OPEC remains in business as usual, and we are not seeing the usual transmissions from Russia against the Chinese and us. Nor against Crimea or Ukraine for that matter. We are pleased with that state of affairs. I would like to show my gratitude by lessening the sanctions a tad against your country. Perhaps your foreign minister and my Secretary of State can get together for a short meeting to establish new guidelines for interaction between our two nations."

"We would welcome such a change, Madam President. Foreign Minister Molokov will be happy to receive State Secretary Willardson's call."

Next, Sybil had a call put through to King Salman bin Abdulaziz Al Saud.

"*As-salaam 'alaykum*," your Majesty," she greeted the elderly man.

"*Wa 'alaykum as-salaam*, Madam President," he responded. "To what should I attribute the pleasure of this call?"

"I wish to tell you face-to-face as one friend to another, that I and my nation thank you for your contribution to the world's economy and to global peace by your continuing royal influence over OPEC's decisions to maintain oil flow in the region."

"It has been my pleasure, Madam President. As always, we greatly value the relationship of friendship between our two nations and between our people."

Shortly after a garden open air brunch, the ODNI [Office of the Director of National Intelligence] contacted Sybil on her secure line. It took several minutes for the security procedures to be authenticated.

"Good morning, Madam President. Minutes ago, we came in possession of some intelligence that will be of interest to you. It came from trusted humint sources, our digital communications officers, and from cooperation with the folks over at the NSA. I grade the information as A+."

"Thank you, Director. What is going on?"

"The North Korean economy is going down the toilet as you well know. They have been coping by denying food and other resources to their minorities, especially in the north. The privileged few surrounding the Great Leader have begun to murmur softly about shortages and about the government's lack of backbone to stick-up for the country against the Great Satan. There have been a few sporadic but very bloody riots and increasing talk of armed insurrection starting from the north and proceeding south. Our beloved Great Leader told his nation on state television for all the hear, that the provocations by America and about the illegitimate government in Seoul have gone too far. Seoul can expect to see the great power of the real government of Korea within a week if sanctions are not eliminated altogether by then.

"The situation is very similar in Iran. The Iranian people have been aware of the direct relationship between American sanctions for several years now. They are becoming increasingly noisy and angry, even in pubic. The pure breed Persians surrounding the Grand Ayatollah in Tehran are apparently feeling the pinch as well now. Grand Ayatollah Khamenei today issued a twenty-eight page proclamation, the gist of which is that the Great Satan will relax its sanctions immediately or else."

Any specifics about what 'or else' includes," the president asked.

"Saber rattling, but the saber in question is nuclear. Khamenei is now claiming that they have more than thirty nuclear armed ICBMs tested and ready to launch. He was speaking to his base followers in his message, but it will certainly get out to the general public and to the foreign news outlets. He states with finality that the nukes have been tested and are operational. He repeated four times that Great Satan will stop its provocations, or it will feel the sting of the 'Thunder-bolts of Allah'.

"He gives us one week to comply."

"Three questions, Director. Are they serious? Are they in cahoots with each other? And are any big brothers on board?"

"Working on it, Madam President. We are hoping to have more information and more concrete information in time for the PDB tomorrow morning, but don't get your hopes up too high, Ma'am. That is a most slippery area of the world and always has been."

President Daniels had her White House staff try to contact Dictator Kim and Great Leader Khamenei; so, she could get a better idea of what the men were really thinking. Both men were out of contact, the staffers learned. It was the same when the intelligence agencies tried their best. There was a veritable black-out of communications with the two rogue nations.

The president got a short report from Dr. Greyshire about the status of the infrastructure project and of the reconstruction efforts. He reported good but slow progress. In response to her direct question, he replied that not a single spadeful of earth had yet been turned west of the Mississippi.

President Sybil Norcroft Daniels did a quick self-assessment and scoring of the issues, concerns, successes, and failures thus far. She graded her administration's efforts as: US v. Saudis and Russians—1 to 0; US v. Iran and North Korea—stalemate, and US v. the issues of reconstruction and infrastructure repair and maintenance–1-+10 in favor of the Congress, the unions, and the opponents in the voting public. It was not her best day.

# CHAPTER THIRTEEN

In November–nearly a year into her presidency–Sybil and her staff had to determine what to continue pursuing and what to wait on. She believed in every issue on her agenda, and to discard or even postpone a full effort for any one of them would be akin to killing of one of her children. Her favorite author had once told her that that was what he felt about cutting sections or characters from his books at the demand of his copyreaders or publisher.

It had been almost eleven months since she first met with Dr. Dastrup and Dr Greyshire and their large infrastructure committee. Thus far, most of the work had been done by volunteers, and that resulted in a huge savings. At least the politicos in the press and members of the legislature could not fault her for extravagance—at least until they made a reckoning of the building reconstruction costs. That project was moving at a rate of swiftness that she had not expected since it was coming out of Washington.

With Dr. Dastrup and his senior committee chairpersons, they made a sober accounting of the sixteen major areas of interest in the repair and maintenance of the nation's infrastructure; so, Dr. Greyshire could get his boots-on-the-ground aspect of the project underway.

The chemical sector was chaired by a savvy professor of chemistry, and head of the department at Yale University, named Donald L. Pietgrass PhD. His committee was succinct, candid, and demonstrated competency not only in planning but in a considerable amount of execution so far.

The chemical sector is an integral component of the US economy that manufactures, stores, uses, and transports potentially dangerous chemicals [by truck, train, pipeline, and airlines] upon which a wide range of other critical infrastructure sectors rely. The chemical sector has a wide base of responsibilities such as prevention of terrorism, security of facilities, transportation of materials including toxic chemicals, maintenance of heavy and light industrial parks, ensuring the purity and quality of chemicals coming from factories that manufacture and transport huge volumes of chemicals—especially thousands of tons of volatile petrochemical feedstocks every day. Another contingent of operatives from the chemical sector is responsible for highly sophisticated laboratories that produce small, but critical quantities of important drugs and other chemicals. They deal with large well-funded start-up companies and small older firms struggling to function in a rapidly changing world.

Dr. Pietgrass's committee submitted an easily understood two-step document which succinctly categorized the vast number of chemicals produced by the chemical sector in what became an excellent reference "Bible" and separately defined each category for a general model describing the sector's supply chain, likely the segment most vulnerable to terrorism and other failures. Dr. Pietgrass and his committee were developing a hand-in-glove positive relationship with the DHS [Department of Homeland Security] and achieved a firm designation of the American chemical infrastructure as a sector of industry critical to public health and safety. DHS contributed funding for earthquake proofing of a great many existing chemical plants and created an atmosphere of critical "all due haste" to get the work done. Pietgrass presented photographs and three short videos to serve as examples of what can be done.

The American Association of State Governors presented a plaque to Dr. Pietgrass praising them for "developing collaboration with federal, state, and local, agencies, identifying essential critical infrastructure workers, plants, and factories and for their work in helping governmental officials in their work to protect their communities, while ensuring continuity of functions critical to public health and safety, as well as economic and national security.

"Dr. Pietgrass's personal contribution was to prepare a list that was extremely beneficial to manage critical infrastructure community decision-making to determine the sectors, sub-sectors, segments, or critical functions, that should receive extra security, be on call to make changes and to produce new products to meet challenges of as yet unknown biological, medical, environmental, and operational, threats to continuing normal operations."

Starting from West to East, the cities of the nation were taking notice of the impressive new infrastructure improvements, and of the increase in employment and economic growth in their regions

The commercial facilities sector infrastructure committee was under the guidance of construction management expert and CEO of Trammell Crow Company, Conrad Finkelstein, with a record of nearly 34,000 developments completed and which served as a model for how a development should be conceived, planned, and constructed with careful management of social and environmental issues, structural integrity, esthetics, access ways, and the best use of land, funding, and materials.

Dr. Finkelstein was a small man, but a dynamo. His employees either loved him or hated him, but always for the same reason; he had an absolute dedication to getting the job done and done right. He was a working man, and he would not ask a man to do anything he was not willing to do. The influence of Homeland Security—including the use of eminent domain when necessary to move things right along—plus the ability to convince sellers to agree to contracts that were as much as 25-40% higher than land values were shortly before the offer came from Finkelstein and Harvey Ross Jensen, Head of Homeland. They were getting whole developments done almost as fast as the think tank could agree on purposes. The planning committee had to race to keep up, and everyone involved was exhilarated.

The dams sector came under the direction of Lt. Gen. Owen Tyler Grant, second-in-command of the army corps of engineers. This sector was probably in the worst shape of any of the critical infrastructure sectors. For example, twenty dams in South Carolina—several over 100 years old—collapsed during rain and floods in 2015. Repairs and maintenance work began on 4,000 of the most dangerous of the 87,000 US dams before any of the other reclamations. Every dam in the country had been subjected to at least annual and often as many as four inspections a year.

Twenty-five states across the US have had headlines of dam failures caused by nuisance wildlife intrusions, and many dam owners find the struggle to manage nuisance wildlife adequately at their dams a never-ending story. A steady work effort had been in progress for three decades to remove rabbit bushes whose roots were powerful and long enough to bore holes all the way through an earthen dam. There had been a similar crusade to get rid of varmints, especially gophers, muskrats, beavers, badgers, prairie dogs, nutria, alligators, armadillo, moles, voles, coyotes, legal livestock, river otter, gopher tortoise, Canada geese, crayfish, and ants. The dams infrastructure army began a sweep of dams from east to west, and a great many people and towns slept easier as they saw the robust beauty of their new or refurbished dams taking shape.

In a similar fashion—but with less speed—the other sectors of infrastructure began to show exciting changes. In many cases, the evidence of infrastructure improvement was only apparent to the people who worked in those critical sectors, including the: commercial facilities, harbors and rivers, communications, critical manufacturing, defense industrial base, emergencies, energy, financial services, food and agriculture, government facilities, healthcare and public health, information technology, nuclear reactors, materials, and waste, transportation systems, water, and waste water systems committees, were working with federal, state, county, and municipal entities to get the work done as well and as quickly as could possibly be done.

Even her opponents in Congress paused long enough in their diatribes against her to give a positive node to Sybil Norcroft Daniels for being the catalyst for the rebirth and regrowth of healthy dams, highways, and other critical sectors, of the nation's foundations.

The following day—the very next day—during a presidential press conference, a Wolf News reporter asked President Daniels if she was aware of a closed door bipartisan special committee meeting scheduled for the following day.

"No, Sir. I have not heard anything about that. I have been pretty busy, as you might be aware."

A *New York Times* White House reporter asked a more blunt question, "Madam President, do you think the Congress might be discussing impeachment proceedings?"

# CHAPTER FOURTEEN

Fourteen senior congressional Republicans and fourteen senior Democrats met in the Capitol Building basement for a "secret" closed doors meeting that was the worst kept secret in the United States that day. Finally–after heavy news reporter pressure–Speaker of the House Shirley Mair Zimbrowski stated that the meeting was a sort of "grand jury". She refused to be more forthcoming. The Senate Majority Leader Ralph Henry Nichols declined to comment.

The air conditioning in the large basement room was on the fritz and only functioned intermittently. The representatives and senators began to sweat within minutes of being seated on uncomfortable folding chairs. Speaker Zimbrowski was the acting chairperson, and she spoke first.

"Ladies and gentlemen, this does not need to be a lengthy meeting. We are here for only one reason and that is to get rid of the worst president in the nation's history. She has been asked to resign; but, no surprise, that is not going to happen. That being the case, we have to use the fine assembled legal minds to develop articles of impeachment. I submit that we have a glaringly apparent first cause: President Daniels went outside and around Congress to obtain a very substantial amount of money from the treasury and flouted it in our faces. If that doesn't qualify as a 'high crime and misdemeanor', I don't know what could."

The Majority Leader was even more brief: "She was never elected, and her behavior is that of a dictator. That is the highest crime the Constitution describes."

The Honorable Steven Handerkopf, Senator from Wyoming, asked, "Do we really have enough evidence of a crime? I mean, doesn't she have a sound Constitutional argument for obtaining the money because of a national emergency, a crisis? I recall quite clearly that the Supreme Court decided in her favor when we challenged her. What else is there, really?"

"Senator, let's get real about this. This is not for publication outside this room. Both the House and Senate transaction in an impeachment proceeding has precious little to do with justice, the law, or even right and wrong. It's politics pure and simple. We politicians want her out because she is bad for us, bad for the Congress, bad for the Constitution, and bad for the people. We need to oust her and get on with real procedures and interactions of United States government. We must be united in that."

Late that morning, the *National Enquirer*, published a second article accusing President Daniels with adultery.

The clincher in the article was a very clear photograph from a long distance telescope using Canon's ridiculously heavy $100,000 1200mm lens.

The DNI informed President Daniels that OPEC had scheduled an emergency meeting of all participating countries for that afternoon with only one item on the agenda: cutting off oil flow from OPEC for the next six months.

Cerisse and Drake's pediatrician diagnosed Sybil and Charles's little grandson, Bonheur, with viral meningitis, and he had to be hospitalized at the WRNMMC [Walter Reed National Military Medical Center formerly known as the National Naval Medical Center] in isolation.

The least bad news of the day for Sybil came from CEO of Trammell Crow Company, Conrad Finkelstein, informing the Infrastructure Committee and President Daniels that the government of California had filed an injunction against the committee and the White House to require them to cease and desist from misusing the doctrine of eminent domain to obtain very preferred land for the committee's development projects. That meant a painful and slow winding pathway through the justice system to the Supreme Court before obtaining a decision. Her lawyers told Sybil that the process could easily take two years. She knew that she might well not even be the president by that time.

By three in the afternoon, Sybil went up to the residence, took a sedative, assumed the fetal position, and turned the electric blanket up to nine.

~ The End ~